EXPECTING
JOY
It's a Girl!

Janene Wolsey Baadsgaard

Bookcraft
Salt Lake City, Utah

Library of Congress Catalog Card Number 99-95577
ISBN 1-57008-705-9

First Printing, 1999

Printed in the United States of America

for my sisters

Chapter One

A WHILE BACK I DECIDED IT WAS about time I did something . . . something that doesn't get eaten up, need rewashing, or follow me around with a runny nose. I'd been putting my personal goals on the back burner for more than twenty years and I had figured that was long enough—even for someone who's a saint or dumb or both. Well, I wasn't no saint or as dumb as I looked. I also figured at the rate I was going, if I kept waiting until I got all my children in school or until my husband was released as bishop, I'd be dead and probably wouldn't feel up to it.

My real wake-up call came when I was talking over the kitchen counter with my daughter Emily, who was about to leave for her morning workout down at that fancy gym next to the Texaco station.

"Mom, you really should start exercising," Emily said with one eyebrow lowered to half-mast as she critically surveyed me up and down. "I bet you couldn't even make it out to the mailbox without getting winded."

"Maybe next week," I answered, bending down to scrub the kitchen floor on my hands and knees.

Then Emily made some comment about a current event in the White House and asked me my opinion on the matter. I answered. Thought my idea on the subject was a real intelligent bit of insight—but she laughed at me. Emily was a college student, so she thought she knew quite a bit.

"Brother, Mom," Emily laughed. "You've been stuck in the house for too many years reading the back of one too many cereal boxes."

I didn't laugh.

Maybe she's right, I got to thinking. *What do I know? . . . Maybe I have read the back of one too many cereal boxes.*

So I decided to do something about it. I never dreamed my planning of a little harmless self-improvement would cause so much trouble. Sometimes, maybe even only one major dramatic time in life, a body just knows what a body's got to do. Nothing short of rigor mortis can stop it.

I sure had a hard time finding Vern to tell him about it though. It's darn right difficult to talk to your husband when he's the bishop, especially when you've got nine children. Vern was either down at the bank writing loans for farmers and ranchers all day or down at the church writing temple recommends or welfare orders all night. Whenever he was home, the kids would keep interrupting us or ward members would call on the phone. If we ever *did* get a moment alone, Vern didn't like to talk much. So, I decided I just couldn't wait any longer. Right after I got the breakfast dishes done, I made plans to *take* my turn, whether anybody gave me permission or not.

"Brother Swenson," I said, balancing the phone between my shoulder and cheek, "LaRue Willey here. Can I make an appointment to visit with the bishop tonight?"

There was a long pause.

"Sure thing, Sister Bishop," Clifford finally managed to mumble. "Got an open spot about eight o'clock . . . Something wrong, LaRue?"

“No, nothing wrong,” I answered. “Do me a favor. Don’t pencil my name in. Just leave me a free time slot, but don’t let Vern know I’m coming.”

“You bet. Sure you’re all right?”

“Never better.”

Later that evening after supervising supper, dishes, baths, homework, piano lessons, reading assignments, and merit badges, I put Jennifer in charge of the younger children and drove down to our chapel. Once inside the church I noticed several metal chairs in the empty hallway next to Vern’s office. I slid into the first chair, trying to ignore the muffled yells coming from behind Vern’s closed door.

Bad timing, I thought. *Vern probably won’t be in such a great mood after getting put in the middle of that war.*

Just then I heard the church entry doors open then slam shut. Two elderly widows from our ward wearing matching polyester floral print dresses and sturdy orthopedic shoes ambled toward me.

“Sister Grayson . . . Sister Ainge,” I said. “You’re both looking fine this evening. How’s the old arthritis?”

“Bearable, bearable, ’cept when it rains,” Sister Ainge answered in a real quivery voice as she grabbed Sister Grayson’s skinny arm to steady her.

“What’s that?” Sister Grayson added, turning up her hearing aid until it squealed. “What’s that you say?”

“I said how’s the old arthritis?” I repeated, much louder that time.

“Old Arthur’s eye test? That’s what you say? Doc says he’s blind as a bat. Not supposed to be drivin’ anymore. Don’t listen. Folks is always honkin’ at us and Arthur waves. Thinks they’s being friendly. Told him a dozen times, they ain’t waving cause they *like* you, Arthur. They’s waving cause they’re mad at ya. But, nooo. He don't listen. Tell him ta let me drive. But nooo. Says I'm too deaf to drive.

"Not Arthur's eye test, Velma . . . ar-thri-tis," Sister Ainge yelled. "Got to speak up, dear," she added at high volume as she turned to me. "Velma don't hear so good no more."

I nodded and smiled.

"*You* gotta wait in line too?" Sister Grayson yelled above the squeal of her hearing aid.

All of a sudden the door to the bishop's office burst open.

"That's it! I'm filing tomorrow!" a middle-aged lady with gigantic false eyelashes and a tight thigh-high skirt yelled as she clomped down the long hall in platform shoes. "You'll never change. I've had it."

"Yeah, well go ahead! See if I care! Not exactly a prize heifer yerself, ya know," a husky male voice boomed from Vern's office.

An enormous bearded man with manure-covered riding boots appeared in Vern's doorway and bellowed down the hall, "See if I care!" Then he turned back toward Vern, adjusted his sweat-stained cowboy hat, and lowered his voice. "'Preciate what yer tryin' ta do, Bishop. Better this way. Had it up to here with her anyhow." He hiked up his worn Rustler jeans then lumbered down the hall toward the exit. "Bet she swiped my truck too, just for spite."

Before Vern had a chance to compose himself, step into the hall, and ask who was next, I jumped up and marched straight into his office, afraid I'd lose my nerve if I didn't act quickly. I sucked in my poochy belly and squared my shoulders. I'd been trying to have a serious conversation with Vern for weeks and I was not going to waste this opportunity for his complete, undivided attention.

As I closed the door behind me, I noticed Vern looked downright handsome in his gray wool suit, starched white shirt, silk tie, and polished boots. Vern's tall and broad shouldered . . . a regular hunk. I felt downright hokey in my white elastic-waist knit pants with threadbare knees. I'd been planning to lose twenty pounds for so long I had almost forgotten why. I'd been pregnant so many times that my stomach muscles had run up the white flag and surrendered years ago. Most of the time my serious attempts to stay attractive didn't seem worth the effort for the outcome. I've got one of those pear figures—ya know—nothing on top but plenty on the bottom. But all that was about to change. Vern did a double take.

"LaRue?"

He never takes my plans for self-improvement seriously, I thought, taking a chair facing Vern's desk. *Why should he? Every time I say I'm going back to school or getting in shape, I find some convenient excuse to quit. I probably hold the world's record for the BYU student who's backed out the most times. Well, I'm* not *going to quit this time!*

"LaRue? What you doing?" Vern asked, obviously uncomfortable with my sudden, unexpected personal appearance in his office.

I noticed Vern's nicely starched shirt. I'd ironed his shirt that afternoon before he got home from the bank so he'd have a fresh one ready to wear. I had dinner on the table promptly at 5:30 like I did every night, so we could eat, then have scripture reading together as a family just in the nick of time for Vern to go to the bathroom, jump up and down three times in the hall, then run down to the church by 6:30 for interviews . . . week after week, year after year.

"LaRue?" Vern quizzed again, peering through

wire-rimmed glasses, his arms resting on the glass-topped walnut desk. "What's wrong?"

"Oh, nothing's wrong," I answered.

"Then what are you doing here? You don't have to make an appointment to talk to me."

"Oh, yes I do. And I got some pretty funny looks waiting in line," I answered, brushing my sweaty hands along the sides of my knit pants. I cleared my throat. What I had to say that night was maybe even the most important speech of my entire midlife crisis and I wanted to get it just right so Vern would take me seriously.

"LaRue?" Vern asked again, with a touch of agitation. I knew most people came to Vern with major marital, financial, or moral problems. Frankly I didn't mind keeping Vern guessing for a minute. At least I had his full attention.

"I've got twenty minutes minimum, right?" I answered.

Then Vern's phone rang. I bolted from my seat and pinned Vern's hand to the receiver.

"Don't . . . you . . . dare . . . answer . . . that," I said, stopping on each word for emphasis.

Vern quickly jerked his hand away from the telephone, cautiously folded his arms across his chest, then leaned back in his chair. But I could tell Vern was still listening for his male clerk to answer the phone in the next room.

"Vern?"

"What?" Vern answered, obviously distracted as he listened to see if he could make out who had just telephoned.

"Good grief, Vern," I finally barked. "Look at me for a minute and pay attention. I have something important I need to tell you."

Vern lowered his eyebrows. "Well then say it. I don't have any time to waste."

I adjusted my glasses, stalling for time. I had that tingly feeling in my nose that always came right before I got emotional. But I knew if I got blubbery Vern would figure it was just a hot flash and tune me out. So I sucked in that nose tingle and plugged off my tear ducts with a surge of sheer willpower that surprised even myself.

"I'm going to go back to BYU to finish my degree," I finally blurted.

"Why?" Vern asked, lowering his eyebrows.

"And I'm going to start jogging with you every morning."

"Why?"

"Because I want to. Because this is important to me."

Vern squirmed around in his chair then stared at the floor, obviously hosting a tug-of-war inside his head thinking about what to answer.

"Fine. If that's what you want to do . . . fine," he finally answered, avoiding all eye contact with me.

"That's all you can say? . . . Fine?" I asked, trying to give him a second chance to say something I needed to hear.

"What do you want me to say?"

"Well, how about, 'Good for you, honey. How can I help you? I'll be there to support you all the way," I answered, rubbing my nose to head off any emotional outburst lurking in the wings.

"Why?" Vern quizzed. "Why now, LaRue? Who's going to tend Christian? Michael's leaving on his mission soon, and Jennifer's wedding's coming up. This just isn't a good time."

"After Jennifer gets married then Emily will," I answered. "After Michael goes on a mission, then Ben will.

It took me a long time to figure this out, Vern, but things are never going to calm down around our house. If I wait any longer to do something for myself, I'm afraid I'll forget who I am and I won't be able to find me when I finally go looking. Maybe we could talk about this as a family, decide what to do—see if I can get some help from you and the kids tending Christian in the evenings. I've signed up for night classes."

Vern lowered his eyebrows again, "Couldn't you just wait for a while? I'll be released as bishop in a few years and Christian will be in school before long and . . ."

I felt my cheeks burn.

"Vern, I've put off finishing my degree for way too many years. There's never going to be a time when everything calms down. I've been thinkin' very seriously about all this. I only have two semesters left if I take a full load. I really think I can do this."

"Yoo-hoo. Anybody home?" Sister Ainge hollered, interrupting us through the closed office door after banging three times. I tried to ignore the interruption while Vern nervously glanced at his office door.

"Vern," I said, trying to recapture his attention. "I was talkin' to Barbara Tolman the other day and she said she got so depressed when she was raising all her kids, all she did was eat donuts and read romance novels for ten years. When she finally went to a shrink, he told her she needed to get out of the house at least once a week and do somethin' for herself, something she liked to do. And you know what happened?"

Vern didn't respond.

"Barbara thought and thought and thought and she couldn't think of even one thing she wanted to do. She *forgot.* Isn't that just the most tragic thing you've ever heard? I don't want that to happen to me."

"Yooo-hooo!" Sister Ainge yelled again while she banged on the door a second time.

"Be right there," Vern answered, looking toward the door.

"Looks like my time's up," I said, hoping Vern would tell Sister Yoo-hoo to hold her darn horses. But Vern didn't say anything, so I knew my time was really up.

As I stood to leave Vern's office, I felt a lonesome pain in the pit of my stomach that crawled up my throat. I swallowed it back down.

"LaRue?" Vern said as I turned to leave. "We'll talk about this when I get home."

"Sure," I answered, exiting through Vern's office door. "Sure."

Sister Ainge and Sister Grayson, not so patiently waiting for temple recommend interviews, peeked through the opened door.

"Bishop!" Sister Grayson yelled above the squeal of her hearing aid. "What's taking so darn long?"

"Bishop Willey?" Sister Ainge added. "Don't mean to interrupt, but Sister Grayson's on a diuretic."

I quickly headed for the east exit of the chapel. I knew Vern wouldn't come after me. After I closed the door of the van and started the ignition, everything that still needed to be done at home—laundry, homework, reading calendars, science fair projects, missionary farewell talks, and Jenny's wedding invitations—rushed into my head and made me feel as if I weighed 987 pounds.

"Oh, grow up and quit feeling sorry for yourself," I said out loud in the van on the way home. "You could have worse problems than being married to a good man who spends all his spare time helping other people and being mother to nine children who need your help every second. This is as good as it gets, baby. So buck up."

Sometimes a body just needs to give itself a good talking to. Can't say it did much good that night though. I felt so lonesome driving home, I couldn't stand it. I stopped on a quiet dark lane, turned off the ignition and head lights, then just kinda poured myself out to God. I'm sure glad Father in Heaven lets us talk to Him when we feel sad—that He doesn't make us get an appointment or wait in line out in the hall. It makes a body feel kinda important.

After that prayer, I wiped my eyes and drove home. Saw no glorious vision, grew no extra set of hands, but deep down inside I felt a new strength and a real deep resolve . . . a peaceful feeling that no one could take away. I knew what I'd planned was all right with me *and* with God and that's all I needed to know.

Chapter Two

"WHAT TIME IS IT?" I CROAKED LIKE a frog with laryngitis.

I'd just heard definite movement near the chest of drawers. Vern, pulling up his sweats in the moonlight from our bedroom window, was almost ready for his ritual morning jog. Vern didn't use an alarm. He woke up at 5:30 every morning, *even* on the first morning of the daylight savings time change.

Vern didn't answer.

"You sure it's morning?" I moaned.

I was stalling for time. I knew Vern would just leave without me if I didn't get my rear in gear and get dressed. Vern had always made it perfectly clear that he didn't have any time to waste.

"My eyes won't open," I moaned as I rolled from our bed with a thud and staggered toward Vern squinting in the darkness. Then I stubbed my toe on the corner of the bed frame and tripped into him.

"Why don't you wear your glasses?" Vern snapped.

"Those stupid things give me headaches and make me feel nauseated," I droned. "I can't get used to them."

Without a word, Vern leaned over the foot board of the bed and stretched the muscles in his leg. I opened and closed my eyes to see if they still worked before I yawned. I'd quit expecting genuine conversation with

Vern when we were alone anymore. Ever since they'd put him in as bishop years ago, Vern's brain and body had seemed to reside in two different hemispheres—a perfectly normal reaction to the impossible job of looking after the needs of five hundred ward members all the time. He grunted after a particularly painful stretch. I stumbled into the bathroom to splash cold water on my face.

"Know what your daughter said to me the other day?" I asked, real serious like. Vern didn't let on if he was listening or not. "She said, 'Mom, why did you settle for being so ordinary? Didn't you ever want to do something important with your life?' . . . How do you figure that, Vern? Kinda made me feel bad she saw me like that. I don't think I'm ordinary.'

My husband, right in the middle of a knee squat, grunted again.

"Vern?"

"Huh?"

"I've spent more than twenty years givin' my whole heart and soul to you and the kids. Then the children grow up and see this overweight housewife who never accomplished anything. You're so busy I don't know if you even see me at all any more." I waited for Vern to say something. He didn't. So I went on, "Well, I told Emily, 'Hey, they gave me the award for having the most children at my last high school reunion.' She just rolled her eyes. I was trying to make her laugh. Then I told her, 'Hey, I gave the world *you.*' She didn't see it. That girl doesn't smile enough, Vern. She's way too focused. How can somebody get straight A's their whole life and not have their personality suffer? You know, I think she'll be too embarrassed to walk around with me when we're both on campus in a few weeks. I can just hear her thinking,

Great, the oldest, dumbest living student in the universe is not only my mother, but now she wants to follow me around campus. . . . Vern, are you listening?"

"Huh?" Vern answered.

"Oh, nothing," I said.

Now don't get me wrong, I genuinely admired people like Vern and Emily. It was just that I had a hard time trying to keep up with them since I really had no desire whatsoever to be focused and disciplined in the first place. Most the time I felt like Vern's live-in speed bump.

"Vern," I said, trying to grab his attention again, "I'd sure like to be more disiplined like you and Emily."

"Why do you say that?" Vern asked.

I knew Vern had watched me start then quit one new self-improvement project after another throughout our whole married life. There was no reason for him to believe this time would be any different. But he had no idea how dramatic I was feeling, or how lonely.

"I'm going to do this. I'm not going to quit, Vern. I know you're just humoring me for a few days 'cause you think I'll quit like all the other times. Well, don't bank on it, buster."

"Don't worry so much about your weight, LaRue," Vern answered.

Weight, I thought. *Did I say anything about weight?*

Vern glanced up, checked his watch, then blurted, "Look, if we don't go now, I'll be late for work. I don't have any time to waste." Then he marched down the hall to finish stretching out on the stairs.

He thinks I'm fat, I thought, glancing down at my rumpled flannel pajamas, hand-me-downs from my older daughters. I couldn't remember when I'd moved from giving hand-me-downs to my daughters to receiving them. *Heaven knows I'm no romance novel cover model.*

Sometimes I would daydream about my life suddenly taking a dramatic turn for the better, like the woman on television who went to the front door in a flowered bathroom towel and plastic shower cap and found out she'd just won the Publisher's Clearing House Sweepstakes. But right that very moment, all my future days seemed to go on and on forever—day after day filled with dishes, diapers, laundry, meals, shopping. I rubbed my eyes and fell back on the bed.

I have to get up and get going or I'll just keep getting fatter and fatter and dumber and dumber, I thought over and over, trying to motivate myself to move.

"Why would any sane person actually want to go jogging at *this* hour?" I muttered to myself in the darkness. "Why would any sane person want to go jogging at *any* hour?"

Then I heard the front door slam shut. Vern was like that. He never waited. I didn't think he meant to be rude, he just didn't see the point of waiting for unmotivated people, like me. I was certain Vern would've knelt across the altar at the Salt Lake Temple without me on our wedding day if I'd been late. I could imagine Vern dressed in white on the temple stairs, shaking his head while I dashed toward the entrance in a dither.

"Sorry, LaRue, you missed it," he'd say.

But today was different. I knew I'd made myself a solemn promise.

"I will exercise at least five days a week and finish my degree in two semesters or I'll die trying," I declared to the hairy black spider on the wall while I pulled up my holey socks. "You can do it," I chanted. "You can do it, LaRuey. You can do it."

I wiggled into my worn blue sweats, clumped down the hall, and stumbled out the front door. Vern had jogged to the stop sign on the road in front of our home and back several times—trying not to get too far ahead. I knew he was trying to be nice by not leaving me in his dust, but somehow that didn't make me feel any better. I knew if I didn't pay very close attention, I'd miss most of Vern's attempts to be nice . . . like the way he picked up milk on the way home from work or kept gas in the van.

I marched down the front steps.

"This is it!" I vowed to myself. "There's no turning back now."

Since this was maybe even the most historic day of my life, I stood on our circular driveway and flung a big two-handed fist high above my head.

"I am LaRue Willey! I will not quit this time!"

I jogged in place for a few minutes, trying to warm up my muscles. My right hip popped, I broke out in a cold sweat, and my heart started beating so loud I thought I'd wake the neighbors.

"This is going to be a little tougher than I thought," I mumbled as I wiped sweat from my forehead. There I was, puffing like an old engine headed up the canyon and I hadn't even left my driveway. I was thoroughly embarrassed with myself.

Then, without thinking—I do that a lot—I looked up at our mountains to the east. Morning sun was lighting up the whole wide sky. Pink, amber, and gold sprayed up from Maple mountain like ripples from a pebble thrown in the pond. I dropped to my knees pretending to tie my shoe laces. A body shouldn't oughta see something like that without thanking God right then and there. So I did.

"LaRue!" Vern yelled as he jogged back past the house again. "What you doing?"

"Praying!" I yelled back. "Just give me a minute. I need all the help I can get!"

“LaRue? You going jogging or not?” Vern yelled back with a totally irritated tone of voice. “I don’t have any time to waste.”

“Coming!” I yelled back. “Be right there!”

We lived on two acres near Spanish Fork. Along the south end of our property there was a long row of old poplars that swayed and creaked in the canyon breeze every morning. People ’round those parts used poplars as wind breaks along their ditch banks ’cause every morning Spanish Fork Canyon whipped out a wind so stiff it tended to blow your socks off and anything else that wasn’t nailed down.

I closed my eyes and listened to my favorite sound in the whole genuine universe—wind washing through my trees like ocean waves against the morning sky. I knew I should be thinking ’bout finally pulling myself together and mustering up the courage I’d never found before. But right when I was going to start jogging, I opened my eyes and saw hundreds of seagulls suddenly swoopin’, soarin’, and divin’ above the newly plowed field across my street. It took my breath away. I was of the firm opinion that God always sent us messages, telling us He loved us every day, but we usually didn’t notice. That morning, I noticed.

“Thanks. I needed that,” I whispered, looking up. “I love you too.”

Suddenly bursting with new energy, I jumped to my feet then hit the road ready to leap over the threshold into a new me. Problem was, pretty soon the old me didn’t seem so bad after all.

This is embarrassing, I thought. *Emily’s right, I can’t even jog to the mailbox without getting winded.*

Turning right, I headed down the road toward my neighbor’s sheep barns. It was a mammoth effort to make it to the first telephone pole.

“You all right?” Vern asked as he doubled back then slowed his pace to stay even with me on the road. “Look a little white. Gonna pass out or something?”

I couldn’t answer. I was barely able to take my next breath. I silently waved Vern forward and tried to smile. Then I stopped on the side of the road and took three deep gasps.

“On second thought”—*gasp*—“maybe I could”—*gasp*—“ride my bike,” I wheezed as I plodded back to the garage. “So you won’t have to keep zigzagging back and forth!”

Once I got up on a bicycle, I had a lot less trouble keeping up with Vern while he was jogging.

“LaRue . . . how . . . can . . . you . . . pedal . . . so . . . slow . . . without . . . tipping . . . over?” Vern yelled as he whizzed past me.

“Yeah, well, all you have to do is put one foot in front of the other. I have to move myself *and* the bike,” I yelled back.

I weaved back and forth on the road, singing at the top of my lungs, “Today while the blossom still clings to the vine, I’ll taste your strawberries, I’ll . . . hummmmmm.” I always forgot that part. “A million tomorrows will all pass away, ere I forget all the joy that is mine today.”

Vern checked behind him to see if any cars were coming, hoping no one had their windows down. I, on the other hand, pictured myself signing a multi-million dollar singing contract someday after all the kids were raised.

Thirty minutes later as we finished our morning workout and approached our driveway, I spied a buck and two does leaping through a barley field up the road a bit. Deer often wandered down from the foot hills near our home and fed in the fields. When the wild animals heard a train roaring down Spanish Fork Canyon, they froze. Like fine music the wild animals held perfectly still then vaulted forward, leaping gracefully over barbed wire fences and irrigation ditches.

"I sure hate the deer hunt," I said, trying to get Vern's attention. "Why would someone want to shoot anybody who looks like Bambi? Ya know, Vern, I heard a story 'bout a cattle rancher who had to back away from a drunk hunter with a rifle once saying, 'All right, I believe you, sir. That's your deer. Just let me get my saddle off her please.' "

I belly laughed. Vern curled his thin lips into a faint smile. I always thought my jokes were a lot funnier than Vern did. All of a sudden like, morning sunlight bathed our whole valley from West Mountain to Maple Mountain, filling up our whole yard with morning light.

I threw back my head, popped my legs out from the pedals, and yelled, "Get ready world! Here I come!"

Vern rolled his eyes and shook his head . . . but I noticed the slightest hint of a smile. I survived on the hope that Vern liked something about me even if he hadn't figured out what it was yet. Problem was, he'd probably never get around to telling me what it was.

Chapter Three

WHEN THE KIDS STARTED BACK TO school at the end of August, the hardest part of my new morning routine was not the workout. The hardest part was getting all the kids fed and ready to catch the bus *after* my bike ride. Mornings at my house would've made good material for those old black and white movies where people looked like they're moving in fast motion and blinking a lot; except I was the only person moving or blinking like that. Everybody else in the family moved in real, real SLOW motion. They totally ignored my standard morning lecture routine that contained the same words repeated three times . . . "Hurry! Hurry! Hurry!"

The only revenge I got was when I yelled "The bus is here!" while one of the children was still in the bathroom with their personality down.

About a week before classes started at BYU I decided I had better check up on my new hangout. After I got all the kids off to school, Christian and I took a bath, played around in the sink, put on makeup, combed our hair with styling gel, then drove over to BYU. It'd been years since I'd been on campus.

After I parked the car, unloaded Christian from his carseat, and walked hand in hand with my one-year-old son past the old Smith Field House, I took one long, slow, deep breath and exhaled. Brigham Young University loomed like some colossal castle high above me at the crest of the hill. Problem was, in order to get there I had to climb a flight of stairs that roughly resembled the Tower of Babel. I wasn't sure Christian and I could make it to the top without passing out. I breathed real deep then started climbing. One by one I climbed each chipped cement step, stopping to help Christian regain his balance and catch my breath after each one.

Maybe I'm just not up to this anymore, I thought. *I can't even make it up the darn stairs to campus. What am I doing?*

Once I got to the top of the stairs, nothing was the way I remembered it. The whole campus looked like it was being reconstructed after World War III. Riding my bike while Vern jogged in the morning was a piece of cake compared to hoofing it around BYU campus. I felt a major twinge in the pit of my stomach. Then I remembered my daughter Katie's nervous questions right before she caught the bus on her first day of school a week ago.

"What if I can't find the bathroom when I have to go? What if my zipper gets stuck? What if the kids laugh at me? What if . . ."

"No matter what happens to you," I'd told Katie, "everything will be all right. 'Cause God watches over you all the time and when you come home, your Mommy will be there and she'll always love you."

No matter what happens to me, I reassured myself as I surveyed the huge campus with Christian tugging on my sleeve, *everything will be all right because God watches over me all the time and when I come home . . . I'll always be there and I'll always love me.*

Funny, but that thought had never dawned on me before—I'd be the only person who'd never leave me. I knew most intelligent people probably figured that out years ago. But that morning the realization of my own constant companionship kinda comforted me.

After a major trek across campus, I pushed open the heavy glass doors and walked into the BYU Bookstore just like I had a right to or something. Felt like I'd walked into heaven. "Hot dog, I love books," I said out loud. I'd almost forgotten that. I couldn't remember the last time I'd been much of anywhere except to our mailbox, Macey's grocery store, first ward church, the orthodontist's office, or one of the local schools. I felt like a baby let loose in a candy store. As far as my eye could see in every direction, there were books—thousands of them. The very smell of them made me feel like soaring. Something inside the dusty cobwebs of my brain woke up.

"Chris," I said, pointing at the rows of books, "look, honey. Look at all those books. Oh, baby, we're in heaven."

For the rest of the morning I bought textbooks, checked with the financial aid office, stopped by the Communications Department, and tried to keep Christian from grabbing every single item off every single shelf we passed along the way. Since I'd dropped out of school to marry Vern, I'd signed up to go back several times. Then, before I knew it I'd find myself pregnant or lose my nerve. Now that I was trying to go back and finish up again, I felt more than a tad foolish. I imagined a sign on my forehead flashing, "Overweight woman having midlife crisis seeks fulfillment and meaning in her dull life by entering school . . . again."

"Is that your grandson?" the cashier asked me while I was paying for a stack of books.

"No. He's my son," I answered. "I'm not as young as I look."

"Is that your grandson?" the Communications Department secretary asked after she handed me the core curriculum schedule.

"Yep, he's grand and he's my son," I smiled back.

"Is that your grandson?" the financial aid officer asked after she helped me with some paper work.

"No, I'm his mother. I know he looks a little young for his age," I answered.

When Christian screamed for his bottle all the way home and I felt so distracted I accidentally ran a stop sign and almost hit a guy on a bike, I started wondering . . . *Maybe all those people are right. Maybe I am a little old for this kind of stuff. What am I doing? Whatever gave me the idea I could handle this? I'm not smart enough. I don't want to neglect the kids or Vern. What in the world am I doing?"*

I felt like racing home with my tail between my legs and immediately doing something safe and domestic like baking bread, tying a quilt, or churning butter. Problem was, I had never in my whole life baked bread, tied a quilt, or churned butter, nor did I ever plan to. Then it dawned on me . . . what was going on inside my head was a pattern. I had to face the real reason I'd dropped out of school so many times before. The real reason I'd never finished my degree was because *I* didn't think I could do it. The battle wasn't just babies, budgets, and husbands—it was *me* and this voice inside my head that said, "LaRue, you're not smart enough; you're not good enough. You'll never be organized enough to handle everything at home and still accomplish something for yourself."

Well, I told that voice out loud, "Shut up! I'm not listening to you any more."

Christian stopped crying. I think he thought I was

talking to him. After I parked the car in our circular drive and walked through the front door, I heard the telephone answering machine click on after the fourth ring, recording the message.

"Hello. Willey Fruit-of-the-Loom factory. We're not here right now, so when you hear the beeper, please be brief."

My children were always putting embarrassing things like that on the answering machine without my permission.

"Hello? Willey's? Nice message you have there. This is the stake president. I'm calling for the bishop. We're having a regional meeting tonight and I want to make sure Vern is there. I'll be down at the stake house if there's a problem. I made this message as brief as possible."

Just as the telephone message finished recording, I heard a car pull up in the driveway and the front door open.

"I've got to run over to the hospital, LaRue," Vern called up the stairs. "I tried to call you but nobody answered. Forgot to tell you but tonight's the stake father/daughter night."

"Oh, Vern. Don't make me go to another father/daughter night," I answered, walking to the head of the stairs. "It's embarrassing."

"Sorry. David's had another heart attack and the family's asked for a blessing over at the hospital right now. I don't know how long I'll be because the doctor told the family he may die any minute. Tell Amber I'm sorry and I'll make it next time."

"Vern, the stake president called. Said to remind you about the regional meeting tonight."

"Guess I won't be home until late. See ya," Vern said, closing the front door behind him.

Well, it looked like Amber was stuck with me for

another father/daughter date. So I decided I ought to at least make the best of things for her sake. Right before it was time to leave, I dressed up in one of Vern's suits, then put on one of those K-Mart Halloween black plastic glasses with hairy eyebrows, a huge plastic nose, and mustache. Then I rang the front doorbell.

"I'm here to pick up my date," I said with the lowest male voice I could muster. "Why, I believe you're the one. Your name's Amber, right?"

Amber couldn't help herself. She busted up laughing so hard, water leaked out her eyes and nose. She took me by the arm and let me open the car door for her. The other fathers and daughters at the stake party looked at us real funny, but we had a blast. I only stepped on Amber's feet about twenty-seven times while we were dancing because I was wearing Vern's shoes.

"I'm sorry Dad couldn't come," I said when Amber and I drove home that night. "Your dad wanted to be here but somebody in the ward had a heart attack and the family asked for him at the hospital and then he had this regional meeting . . ."

"It's all right, Mom."

Amber was never that quiet. I knew something was wrong.

"Sometimes I wish Dad weren't the bishop," Amber finally said, breaking the silence. "At first I thought it was cool, like my Dad's the boss . . . but now I wish he weren't the bishop 'cause he's gone all the time."

"I miss him too," I said. "I guess it should make us feel better knowing he's helping people with really big life and death problems. Maybe you could figure you have a hand in helping the sick or sad people in the ward too because you're letting your dad help them."

“I guess,” Amber answered. “But I still miss him, Mom. I still wish he were here.”

“I know,” I answered. “Me too.”

“Guess what?” I said, trying to change the subject. “I’m going back to school.”

“Why do you want to do that, Mom? I’m going to celebrate when I finally get out of school.”

“Because that’s what I want to do,” I answered. “Because that’s what I’ve *always* wanted to do. Graduating from BYU was a goal I set for myself when I was your age. If I don’t do it, I’ll let myself down big time.”

“Then go for it,” Amber answered. She thought for a minute, then a huge smile spread across her face. “Way to go, Mom.”

Chapter Four

WHEN BYU STARTED FALL SEMESTER classes the day after Labor Day, I felt like a race horse pawing at the starting gate—only I had one small problem. Ten people had ropes around my neck trying to hold me back. All I wanted to do was attend my first honest-to-goodness college credit class in over twenty years. You never heard so much moaning and groaning in your life. You'd have thought I wanted to fly to the moon or run down the street naked.

Vern had interviews scheduled down at the church all night. Jennifer had back-to-school night. Emily said she had some important errands to run. Michael had the two-to-ten shift at Macey's. Amber had Young Women's and Ben and Aaron had Scouts.

"Wait a minute here!" I hollered as everybody charged from the dinner table, leaving me alone with the dishes to wash and Alisa, Katie, and Christian to tend. "Just wait a minute every one of you! I want everybody back around this table this minute."

"Look, LaRue, I've got appointments in ten minutes. I haven't got any time to waste," Vern huffed.

"Mom," Ben groaned. "I've got to get ready to go."

"Now," I repeated. "I want everybody back around this table, now!"

After the most melodramatic feet dragging you've ever seen, I finally reassembled my family.

"I have a seven o'clock class in Provo," I said matter of factly. "That means I need to leave by 6:30. I need someone to stay home and take care of Alisa, Katie, and Chris. Any volunteers?"

It was deathly silent.

"Why do you have to go to class?" Aaron piped up. "You're too old to go to school. You're not that dumb. Why don't you just stay home and do the dishes and tend the little kids like you always do?"

"Because my brain is turning into mush, that's why. Anybody have any suggestions about how we can make this work?"

"Look, I'd help, but I've got to go," Vern said as he turned and walked down the hall for his briefcase.

"Wait, Dad, I need a ride to the church!" Ben yelled.

"Me, too," Aaron added as they both followed their father.

"I'm supposed to be there too," Amber said. "We're working on personal progress tonight in Laurels."

"Well, I'm working on the personal progress of LaRue Willey and I want a little support!" I said to no one just after I heard the front door slam shut.

Suddenly there I was at the dinner table, stacked high with an atomic bomb blast of food and dishes along with Christian, Katie, and Alisa. I needed to be over at BYU in forty minutes. I knew none of the girls in the ward would be able to baby-sit because they had Young Women meetings and all the boys had Scouts. I was not going to let anything depress me, not this time.

I loaded the dishwasher, cleaned up Katie and Alisa, then changed Christian's diaper with lightning speed. Then I packed a bag with books, treats, toys, diapers, and wet-wipes. After all three children were loaded in the van, we drove to campus. As I walked inside the gleaming glass Tanner building for my first class, Statistics 552, I had Christian dangling on one hip, Katie squeezing one hand, a bag of treats in the other, and Alisa holding onto my skirt with one hand while she sucked her thumb. Wasn't exactly what I'd been dreaming about.

Once I found the classroom and walked inside, it was noisy and crowded so no one noticed me or the kids much. I was hoping the teacher had planned a quick overview of the course with handouts for the evening and would let us go early. I rolled out a quilt and spread the books, toys, and blankets for the kids at the next to the last desk on the last row at the top of the lecture hall, where I would be the most hidden. The classroom was one of those new carpeted lecture rooms with rows of desks on tiers sloping downward toward the blackboard at the bottom of the hall.

"Shhhh," I warned before the teacher came in. "Alisa, try to keep Christian quiet. Let him play with my old jewelry and give him his bottle if he starts to make noise."

BYU required all communications majors to take a statistics class and this was the only one taught at night. Problem was it was a graduate level course. I hadn't had any math since Algebra I and Geometry in high school, so I knew I was in for a brain burner. After the teacher walked into the room and took his place at the front of the lecture hall, I felt my heart race. I knew there was probably some rule against taking children to class, but I had learned from past experience that it's easier to ask for forgiveness than permission.

"Good evening, I'm Dr. Bellows," the professor droned, a downright serious sort of fellow. "I am the instructor for Statistics 552. If you're in the wrong classroom, please feel free to leave at this time."

So far so good. I got a few weird stares from the student sitting next to me but the children were quiet so far.

"In this class we will cover all the formulas you need to know to assist you with your graduate research. If you're looking for an easy A, you're in the wrong class. I require focus and discipline."

I gulped. Then the teacher handed out a student manual that went along with the assigned text and explained homework policy, test scoring, and how he computed grades. Next he adjusted his tie, turned off the lights, and began his first lecture using the overhead projector.

I was in luck. I could pick up Christian and feed him his bottle without anybody seeing me.

For no reason whatsoever Christian yanked the bottle out of his mouth and started yell-singing at the top of his lungs, "Do Wah, Do Wah, Do Wah!" over and over again. The professor stopped lecturing when all the students burst into laughter.

"We do not allow children in the classroom," the teacher stated with an air of disgust. "Whoever you are, please be so kind to step out of the hall with your child at this time. Do not come into my classroom again unless you are able to hire the services of a qualified baby-sitter."

I was so embarrassed I almost melted from cheek flush right there. "I'm sorry," I answered, gathering up my three children. "I won't let this happen again."

"Do Wah! Do Wah! Do Wah!" Christian sang again, breaking the class into laughter once more.

After we left the building through the west exit, I plopped down on the grass next to a maple tree outside the building.

“You guys can be as noisy as you want now,” I said, pulling Katie and Alisa toward me and hugging them.

“Christian was trying to sing the sandman song like you always sing him when you’re putting him to bed, Mommy,” Alisa said. “When they turned out the lights and you gave Christian his bottle, he thought you were putting him to bed and you forgot to sing his song.”

“Oh,” I said. “Of course.”

I took little Christian into my arms and started singing his favorite lullaby, “Sleep tight, sandman’s a-comin’ and he’ll be here mighty, mighty soon and if you don’t cry, he’ll be coming by with a great big lollipop moon . . . How I love my little Christian, sweet and precious little Christian. How I love my little Christian, honest to goodness I do.”

“Do Wah! Do Wah! Do Wah!” Christian answered, snuggling his blond head into the crook of my arm.

Well, even though my first class didn’t turn out like I expected, it didn’t take me long to figure out how to solve my “no family support” problem. I no longer *asked* for volunteers, I made assignments. I masterminded an elaborate Willey family schedule after that first evening class disaster. Everybody moaned, but I wasn’t about to use that as a reason to quit or not expect help. Nothing was going to stop me. Not then, not ever. I taped a giant weekly calendar on the front of the refrigerator with the hours blocked out for each day of the week with a different family member assigned each evening for baby-sitting duty. No one seemed too upset because I also offered cash and treat incentives to anyone caught helping their mother on the sly.

If I thought getting the family to help me was hard, I hadn’t even considered the impossible task of taking physical education for the first time in twenty-five years.

Everyone who graduated from BYU was required to take Fitness for Life, a course designed to help students figure out a personal fitness plan and stick with it . . . for life. I was hoping since I'd already lived half my life, the instructor would let me put in half the effort. No such luck.

If you want to feel old, go back to school when you're the middle-aged mother of nine. If you want to feel ancient, enroll in PE 129. This class curriculum was specifically designed to tell people how fat and worn out they were. Now, I already knew how fat and worn out I was and I didn't appreciate someone rubbing it in. When my instructor, alias Fitness Fred, stood in front of my first physical education class in over several decades and said he was going to make us all run eleven laps on the inside track of the Smith Fieldhouse, I decided to plead medical hardship. I approached him before the timed run with my speech mentally prepared.

"I've just crawled off the delivery table, after nine difficult pregnancies," I pleaded. "Surely you can't mean for me to run eleven laps."

"Does your family have a history of sudden heart attacks?" instructor Fred asked in reply.

Now I wasn't worried about my family history at that moment. I was worried about mine. But I answered truthfully. "No," I replied.

"Run the laps," Mr. Fitness said with a stone serious face. "You will feel pain, and I don't mean the childbirth kind."

I swallowed hard then set out for the Smith Fieldhouse. The indoor track was jam-packed with young men and women who looked like they could run forever without getting the least bit winded or sweaty. I, on the other hand, hadn't even worn a pair of shorts for over twenty years. Reluctantly I rolled up my pants, which instantly exposed my white razor-stubbled legs, granny anklets, and orthopedic shoes. I approached the track breathing deeply. Taking a quick look at the clock next to the women's restroom, I began my timed run.

I got about halfway around the first lap before I totally ran out of gas. *Just ten and a half left to go,* I thought. *Piece of cake, LaRue. Go for it, big Rue!*

That was the last time I was coherent for the duration of the ordeal. Lack of oxygen can do strange things to an otherwise—at least sometimes—normal brain.

Please, you guys. Just one more step, I pleaded with my legs.

I gave it every ounce of courage and determination I possessed. Without totally stopping—sometimes I walked and limped—I lived through the entire Herculean marathon. I dragged my barely breathing body over the finish line feeling pretty good about myself. At least I didn't die. After a very lengthy cool down, I grabbed my class manual and looked for the chart that would tell me my fitness rating.

The manual read, "If you ran 1.5 miles in . . ." I filled in my time ". . . your fitness category is . . . Pathetic."

I was so deflated, I sunk to the track floor in a heap. But even as bad as that timed run was—at least I didn't have to do it in front of the whole class. The next time I showed up for class, I couldn't believe what the instructor expected me to do.

"Today, class, we will measure the fat content of your body, weigh you, and record your height. As I read your name, please line up in alphabetical order."

The first order of business was fat pinching. While standing in line waiting for my turn to get pinched, I remembered the chocolate mint ice cream with raspberries on top I'd eaten for supper that night. My instructor took out a device that looked as if it had been invented when prison torture was legal in this country. When I reached the head of the line, my instructor noticed I looked a bit nervous.

"Nothing to it. Just step right up here," the instructor said while he grabbed me around the arm and pulled me toward him. "This is simple and painless. We need to find out what percent of your body is made up of fat."

"That's private," I pleaded.

My instructor chuckled as if I was trying to be funny or something while he grabbed hunks of my side, thigh, and arm. Then he wrote a bunch of numbers down on a piece of paper and told me I was dismissed.

The next part of this humiliating class period consisted of being weighed and measured. It was not enough to know you're cardiovascularly pathetic and that a large part of your body consisted of fat—now I also had to find out how short I was and how much I weighed in front of an entire class of beautiful people half my age who tended to stand in groups a lot and snicker.

After my teacher gave me all this useful information about myself, he told me and the rest of the class that we had to do something about it or we'd fail the class. We had to mark down the type of exercise we wanted to commit to, the duration of the workout time—then do it five days a week for the rest of the semester.

"You *must* show progress," the instructor said without a smile. "We will repeat the timed run, the fat measure, and weighing in at the end of the semester. That's sixteen weeks. If you show no improvement, you fail this class. Is that clear?"

No improvement, no passing grade. Well, I thought, *at least it won't take much for me to show improvement. It's all uphill from where I sit.*

My plan to exercise with Vern every morning was exactly what I needed to fulfill the requirements of the class; it was like I was hitting two birds with one winded rock.

After class that night, I walked slowly down the long cold tile hall toward the exit of the Richards Building a little discouraged to say the least. Near the front of the building was a very large, serious portrait of Stephen L Richards next to a plaque in bronze that read, *The human body is sacred—the veritable tabernacle of the divine spirit which inhabits it. It is a solemn duty of mankind to develop, protect, and preserve it from pollution, unnecessary wastage and weakness.*"

"I'm working on it," I said as I shuffled from the building. "I'm working on it."

Chapter Five

ANYONE WHO THINKS SUNDAY IS A day of rest has never been a Mormon bishop's wife with nine children. Though I was determined to keep the Sabbath day holy so I could ask for God's help the rest of the week, sometimes I wondered if I would survive another Sunday without completely losing my marbles.

Early one Sunday morning in October I was in my bedroom trying to read the scriptures when out of the blue I suddenly realized two of my children were *really* leaving home in a few weeks. Now, I wasn't dumb. I knew Jennifer had been engaged for months. I'd helped her pick out a wedding dress, choose invitations, gone to her bridal sitting, addressed envelopes, ordered food and flowers. I knew Michael had received his missionary call to Germany weeks ago. I'd helped him buy ten white shirts, two suits, ten pair of socks, an overcoat, shoes, luggage, passport picture, and doctor/dentist exam. But as I was sitting there that Sunday morning it hit me like a left jab straight through the heart that my job description was about to change without any permission. I was going to miss my children immensely.

I knew my Jenny and Michael weren't being dropped off the face of the earth, but in a few short weeks I wouldn't see them when they woke up in the morning or be able to peek at them in the middle of the night. The window of their childhood was closing and I wasn't ready. It seemed like the length of time since the moment I'd brought Jenny and Michael home from the hospital had been roughly twenty minutes. Now they were leaving. I was so sad and glad all wrapped up together that all I could do was bawl. I highly recommend bawling . . . it lets you feel what you're feeling without getting it stuck in your throat. A deep down thankfulness for the gift of my children filled me up till I couldn't leave the feeling inside . . . so I let it out.

Baby Christian, who had been playing with his plastic jungle animals next to my feet, looked up at me confused and insisted, "Look at me!" He stood and tugged at my leg, obviously bewildered with my emotional outburst. "Look at me, Mommy!"

I slowly picked up my year-old son and wrapped my arms around him. Then I turned his pudgy wet face to mine and looked at him, like it was the first time—felt the miracle of him. His childhood was passing too.

"Mom! Katie's gonna stick her knife in the toaster," Alisa screamed from the kitchen. When you're the mother of nine, reflective moments don't last for long. I raced toward the kitchen with Christian still in my arms.

"Katie," I yelled. "Don't you know you can't do that? You'll electrocute yourself."

"Told you," Alisa sneered.

"What's electrocute, Mom?"

"That means *you'll* turn into toast."

Sundays always gave me the feeling that I was herding marbles uphill—most likely the ones I'd lost. That particular Sunday was no exception. No matter how fast I worked all morning making breakfast, doing the dishes, getting the younger children dressed with hair combed, ties tied, and diaper changed, along with getting myself presentable and assembling a giant bag of lesson manuals, scriptures, Primary talks, snacks, and drawing pencils and paper, one particular child always insisted on playing the role of cold molasses getting out the front door.

Every Sunday since before the flood our entire family, minus one particular child, would sit in the van and wait.

"Just leave him. It'll teach him a lesson."

"I have to be there early to set up chairs in the Primary."

"I'm supposed to help get the sacrament ready."

"Well, if we're just going to sit here, I'm going back in the house and watch TV."

"No one is leaving this van without my permission," I would declare, checking my watch again. "Unless you want to face the firing squad."

I tried not to drug myself before we left for church, or murder one of the children, but it took a great deal of self-control. I always felt like I'd been through a marathon with my head on backward. The faster I ran, the more behind I got. Sometimes I wished Vern could be home on Sundays to help, but then I'd remember that his favorite pre-bishop Sunday activity had been sitting in the chair holding the priesthood.

Well, after cold molasses finally jumped into the car that Sunday, we peeled from the driveway in a cloud of smoke. The policeman in town had told me he wrote most his tickets on Sunday for people speeding to church when they're already late anyhow. I finally settled the family into a long row near the back then checked to see if I'd remembered everything. I had my Relief Society materials ready for my lesson, paper and pencil for the younger children to keep them quiet during the sacrament service, my scriptures, secret sister present for Amber in Young Women, a diaper and bottle for Christian just in case and . . . what was I forgetting?

"Mommy, you forgot my talk," Alisa said, pulling on my sleeve. I remembered setting Alisa's Primary talk and pictures on the kitchen counter so she wouldn't forget them.

"We'll have to think of another talk real fast," I whispered. "It's called ad libbing. Don't worry. I'll come in the Primary room and help you."

Oh brother, another ad lib Primary talk, I thought.

Vern was conducting that month, which meant he would be bearing his testimony first before he turned the time over to the congregation. *Maybe he'll say something nice about me,* I thought. *Husbands usually say how much they love their wives on fast day.*

During the sacrament service, Vern closed his eyes. I knew he was reverently shutting out distractions so he could be more spiritually in tune. Just as I was about to close my eyes, Katie pulled a colored pencil from the bundle held together with an elastic band from my canvas church bag. The elastic caught the pencil just long enough for Katie to launch the pencil across the entire width of the chapel straight into Brother Anderson's unsuspecting forehead right between the eyes.

Even though I rolled my eyes into the top of my head, trying to pretend I was totally oblivious of the deed, the rest of my children got the giggles. I looked up at the stand and saw Vern, his eyes still closed, most likely receiving inspiration for his testimony. After the sacrament service was complete, Vern stood to begin the testimony bearing part of the meeting. I mentally repeated the same words over and over in my head, *Please say you love me, Vern. I need to hear you say you love me.*

I don't know why I got so dramatic and set myself up like that. It wasn't healthy, I was sure of it. Maybe it's because a good share of the people in our ward figured I was a single mother. Vern always looked so handsome and spiritual in his Sunday suit with his broad shoulders and angular masculine face—I just couldn't help myself.

Next thing I knew, Vern walked to the podium and began his testimony. I listened very carefully while Vern spoke about his love for the gospel and Christ's Atonement and how much joy his children brought into his life. "And I just have to say how much I love . . ."

He's going to say it, I thought, trying to hold back tears. *He loves me, he really does.*

"Bill, Leon, and . . ."

Bill, Leon? I thought, confused.

"Susan."

Susan . . . Susan? My name's not Susan. Who's Susan? Is this some kind of confession?

"It's so great to work with these guys."

About thirty seconds after Vern sat down, it dawned on me that he had been talking about his counselors in the bishopric and the Relief Society president.

"Mommy," Katie said, pulling on my sleeve again. "How come they call this fast Sunday? It's real slow to me."

I wrapped my arm around Katie and whispered in her ear, "Seems real slow to me too, honey."

For the rest of the meeting I let myself cry without feeling the least bit self-conscious 'cause fast Sundays in our ward generally included a lot of eye dabbing and nose blowing from most members, especially the female kind.

"Mom, Brother Gibson will bear his testimony now," Amber whispered matter-of-factly in my ear. Amber sat next to me through the entire meeting and continued to whisper who would bear their testimony next before the individual ever moved a muscle to stand and walk to the microphone.

“How do you do that?” I whispered, flabbergasted.

“It’s not hard, Mom,” Amber answered. “The same people bear their testimonies in the same order every month.” I wondered why I’d never noticed that.

After our marathon three-hour block of meetings, I drove my boys around in the van to collect fast offerings. Vern would use this money for the needy in our ward, which included families in seventy-five rental units and half-a-dozen blocks of homes. By the time we got home, the older children were so faint from their twenty-four-hour fast or edgy from the inability to move at church for three hours, they either went to sleep or started fighting.

I helped the younger children out of their church clothes, changed the baby’s diaper, then fixed something for everybody to eat. Alisa spilled a bowl of tomato soup on the rug and Aaron stepped on a slice of cheese-covered bread. As soon as their tanks were filled, the children magically disappeared. I sat at the table and looked over the war zone heaped on the dining room table. I didn’t have the energy to find the child who was supposed to be in charge and make them do the dishes. I didn’t have the energy to do the dishes myself. I didn’t have the energy to finish eating the piece of bread in my mouth.

I had had it. Sometimes, like earlier in the day, I felt downright warm, soft, and sentimental about my life with a house full of children. Sometimes, especially by the end of a long hard Sunday, I didn’t. I finished the dishes, then staggered down the hall, ready to collapse in the recliner. From the corner of my eye I noticed water leaking from the bathroom door. I shook the door, but it was locked. “Who’s in there?” I yelled. “What’s going on?”

Then I heard Aaron’s muted whimper. “The toilet’s flooding.”

“Let me in!”

"No, you'll get mad at me."

I quickly lowered the volume of my voice, trying not to sound upset. "Let me in. I won't get mad," I said, totally faking my intense urge to scream as water continued pooling around my feet. Slowly the door squeaked open and a giant wall of water fell out. The entire bathroom floor was flooded.

"What have you done?!"

"See, I told you you'd get mad at me."

"For Pete's sake try to make the water quit flooding! Take the lid off the back of the toilet! Hold that little doohickey up or down or something!"

"I don't know how. See, I told you so. You're mad at me," Aaron cried.

"Throw the towels down and start mopping things up! For Pete's sake help me!" I yelled as I waded through the foul water to find the doohickey.

Aaron was paralyzed. His eyes glazed over. He refused to move. He cried harder. "You're mad at me! You're mad at me!"

Just as I threw a towel toward Aaron, I slipped. I felt the back of my head whack the towel bar on my way down. Aaron lunged for the towel and hit his head on the edge of the toilet. A giant blue welt formed under his eye. We both looked like we'd been in a water polo boxing match.

After mopping, disinfecting, and reshowering, I collapsed in a chair thirty-seven seconds before Vern walked through the door from church.

"So this is what you do all day while I'm gone," Vern teased.

I did not smile—not even a little.

"Vern, just once I wish you could be here when you're not home to see how it is when you're not here."

Then the phone rang. Even though Vern was home in body, he would be talking on the phone to someone in the ward for most the night or coming and going to solve problems or give blessings. By the end of the day, Vern was so exhausted, he went straight to bed without a word and was snoring before I could wrap up things around the house.

Before I went to bed, I glanced into the study and noticed the wall of my ancestors' photos. I felt so guity. I knew my pioneer kin had things so much harder. Those brave pioneer ancestors of mine had probably never complained or gotten mad at their kids or cried or anything like that. They'd lived in mud huts while they built temples; they'd walked across the plains to the Salt Lake Valley in bare bloody feet; they'd fought the Indians bare-handed; they'd known the true meaning of sacrifice and heroism. I was sure they'd died without ever uttering one cross word or entertaining one tiny bad thought. Their husbands had gone on foreign missions and left them alone for years with huge families to care for. My great-grandmothers not only had to share their bishop husbands with over five hundred ward members, they had to share their husbands with other wives.

I knew, without a doubt, I was one gigantic sniveling poop that didn't deserve the celestial kingdom, not ever, not in this lifetime, or the next. I couldn't even handle one little inconvenience like a flooding toilet. Why, what my ancestors would have given even to have an indoor toilet! I knew I was the most ungrateful, impatient, rotten, good for nothin' woman in the history of Mormondom. It was all I could do to make my body move, slop into my bedroom, then undress with the faint light from the closet.

"Maybe you should pass out applications at church for a new bishop's wife," I said after I slipped into bed.

“Why’s that?” Vern mumbled, still mostly asleep.

“I didn’t handle things very well today,” I complained.

“You don’t have to handle things,” Vern yawned as he rolled over.

“What do you mean?”

“Just muddle, LaRue. Trust me. Smile like you know what you’re doing, then just muddle through. No one will ever know the difference.”

“You don’t muddle, Vern. You have everything under control all the time.”

“Sure got you fooled,” Vern yawned.

After he said that I actually wondered for the first time if Vern ever felt as overwhelmed and underqualified as I sometimes did. It had never occurred to me that Vern could ever feel incompetent. He’d never even hinted of it before. It didn’t seem possible. He had always seemed so—well—in control of himself and every situation.

“Vern, I have my first test tomorrow,” I said. “I’m scared to death.”

“I can tell,” Vern answered. “Do you think you could let go of my arm? You’re cutting off the circulation. It’s going numb.”

“I don’t know if I can do it. Do you think I can do it? Do you think my mind’s mud after all these years?”

“Oh, LaRue, you’ll do fine,” Vern answered.

Then, after exactly three seconds, I heard Vern snort, then break into a full-blown snore. I was timing him by the clock on our night stand.

“Three seconds before meltdown,” I mumbled. “A new Vern record.”

Chapter Six

"MAYBE IT'S PSYCHOLOGICAL," VERN stated flatly early Monday morning. "Subconsciously, you don't *really* want to go back to school or exercise, so you get sick."

I finished throwing up, reached for a cold wash rag, then staggered to the bed. Vern patted me on the shoulder, then left the master bedroom to begin his ritual stretching and jogging routine. The wet rag felt cool on my forehead as I closed my eyes to make the room stop spinning.

"Mom, I need this permission slip signed," Ben said, pushing a piece of paper into my green face.

"I can't write with my finger," I mumbled. "Get me a pen."

Jennifer stormed into the room with hot rollers stuck all over her head, resembling an extraterrestrial ready to pick up radio signals.

"Emily thinks she has more right to use the car than I do," Jenny said. "She won't adjust her schedule but she expects me to. I put more gas in it than she does and she always stinks it up with her sweaty gym clothes. Tell her I need the car too."

"If you girls are going to fight over the car, you can both take the bus."

"Mom? Katie just spilled milk all over the kitchen floor!" Alisa yelled.

“Somebody get in there and help her wipe it up. I don’t feel well,” I answered, holding my head.

“Mom,” Ben said, “here’s the pen. Sign it quick.”

“Mom, I need my hair combed,” Alisa pleaded.

“Mom, I can’t find my shoes,” Amber added.

“Mom, didn’t you wash my gym clothes?” Aaron asked.

“Mom, I need lunch money,” Alisa pleaded. “The lunch ladies keep putting red punches on my hand.”

“Mommy, I put the bread in the toaster, but it won’t flush,” Katie cried.

I moaned, then staggered from the bedroom down the hall using the walls for support. Monday mornings were always like this. I managed to write two checks for lunch money, locate substitute gym clothes, comb several heads of hair, wipe up the milk in the kitchen on my hands and knees, and trip over Aaron’s Roller Blades in the hall before I had to find my way back to the bathroom.

“Prayer time,” I heard Vern yell from the living room after he’d come back from his morning jog, showered, and dressed for work. I still had my head over the toilet.

I crawled into the living room on all fours then knelt down at the side of the couch, using a cushion to support my head. Slowly each child wandered into the front room in various stages of dressing.

When all eleven family members were ready, Vern called on Katie to pray. Vern usually called on the younger children when he was running a little late because their prayers were always blessedly short.

“Heavenly Father,” Katie began, “thanks for the nice day and help us not to fight and hit each other and have a good spirit and tell Ben not to tease me anymore and name of Jesus Christ, Amen.”

After the prayer, I rolled onto the couch and took a deep breath.

"Wave to me, Mom."

"I have to work tonight after school so I'm taking the car," Amber said as she left.

"Anything you need from town?" Vern asked as he pecked me on the cheek and headed down stairs.

"Just a friend," I mumbled.

"Huh? What'd you say?"

"Oh, nothing."

When all the children were safely out the door or on the bus, I felt like crawling back in bed and pulling the sheets over my head.

"Mommy, Mommy, Mommy, I do poop!" Christian said over and over until I looked him right in the eye and praised him.

"Good boy, Christian. Good boy do poop. Let's go change your diaper."

If this is the flu, I hope it's the twenty-four-hour kind, I thought.

Then it dawned on me—I was late. There was so much going on with my university classes, Jenny's wedding, and Michael's missionary plans, I hadn't noticed. I checked my planner for dates and shook my head.

No, it couldn't be. Maybe this is the beginning of . . . the big change or something.

More than a tad nervous, I checked the yellow pages and found out who gave free pregnancy tests on Monday afternoons just to make sure. Before I went to my classes that evening, I slipped into a doctor's office in Provo.

After waiting for a few minutes, a nice young nurse at the doctor's office called me by name and asked me to step into the back room where she said, "Mrs. Willey, I'm happy to inform you that your pregnancy test is positive."

I stared at her.

"Are you sure? Are you absolutely sure? I think I'm too old for that."

"I'm sure," she smiled, pointing to the test results on the counter. "You can see for yourself. I get that reaction a lot. Do you want me to write down your due date?"

"Are you sure?" I asked again.

The nurse just smiled.

"Your due date is May fifteenth. Congratulations, Mrs. Willey."

I was speechless. We'd already had our late-in-life surprise, and then six years later, our late-in-life shock. I walked out to the parking lot in a daze. All of a sudden I laughed so loud, the lady passing me jerked to stare at me.

"What's so funny?" the lady in the parking lot asked.

"Life," I said, looking up as I crawled into my van. "Life."

I had a hard time focusing on my test that evening. I kept getting sidetracked inventing humorous or dramatic speeches to tell Vern he was about to become a new father at forty-five on top of everything else. That's probably why I was the last student in my class to hand in the test. The professor kept drumming his fingers and checking the clock on the wall while he waited for me to finish.

When I got home from class, I was so tired I could barely move. My only goal in life was to collapse on the bed and sleep for about two zillion years. But as soon as I opened the front door, Vern met me at the head of the stairs acting real nervous.

"LaRue, a lady wants me to meet her at the church right now and I'm not supposed to meet with a woman down at the church alone. Would you come with me? None of my counselors are home."

"I really don't feel well, Vern. Do you have to meet with her right now?"

"Yes, I have to meet with her right now and I can't tell you why. Can't you pull yourself together? Look, I don't have time for an argument. Are you coming or not?" Vern asked.

"All right," I answered. "Can I go to the bathroom first?"

Vern listened to a sobbing lady for over an hour while I sat in the ward clerk's office reeling with nausea. I had to rush to the lady's room twice. I was asleep with my head on the desk when Vern finally came and got me after the woman left.

"So, how'd things go?" I asked, trying to brighten us both up after we climbed back into the car and started home.

"It's confidential," Vern answered, his eyebrows pinched together in a tense draw. Then that long, hard silence followed.

Those two words had a way of making me feel like we were living together but our hearts were twenty zillion miles apart. Vern couldn't share ward member confessions under any circumstances. I understood and respected that. It wasn't his fault or my fault—it was just part of the job description. Maintaining confidences between ward members and their bishops was a sacred trust, we both knew that. But our inability to talk about the very things that were weighing on Vern the most had a way of creating a vast wall of silence between us—a huge ravine without a bridge.

After we pulled into the driveway, Vern marched straight into the house without saying a word. I could tell he was deeply troubled by the interview and wanted to be left alone. I wanted to tell him about the new baby but the timing didn't seem right. I walked around to the backyard, trying to figure out how to help Vern without knowing what burden he was carrying.

Then I remembered the clubhouse Vern had built for the children a while back and I decided to sit out there a spell and collect my wits. I snuck in the garage and rummaged around until I came up with a sleeping bag, an old camping pillow, and a flashlight. The clubhouse was creaking in the wind real spooky-like as I crept around to the front opening and threw my sleeping bag and pillow inside the small enclosed room roughly six feet off the ground.

"If anybody happens to be running around up there, look out 'cause here I come," I announced to the darkness. "You better scoot out of here real fast because I have my mouse-munching machine and I'm just itching to splat something."

Then I climbed the ladder to the clubhouse with the flashlight in my teeth. When I got inside, I unrolled the bag and slowly unzipped a space with just enough room to climb in. Flashing a beam of light into every corner of the room, I took one more quick look around for any uninvited guests.

Vern hadn't finished enclosing the clubhouse yet and I could see the night sky through openings in the plywood walls. Disappearing and reappearing through the clouds, the moon made grotesque shadows rise and fall all around me. I heard the neighbor's dog bark then bark some more. It felt good to think without a hundred interruptions. A long while later I heard rustling in the apple trees and steady footsteps coming toward me. The hair on the back of my neck rose.

"I don't know who you are but you better get out of here quick! Me and my husband are sleeping out here with the huntin' rifle and we know how to use it!" I warned.

There was complete silence for a moment; then I heard the footsteps start up again, only this time moving more slowly and carefully. Suddenly a huge hairy paw reached into the clubhouse and grabbed my foot. I screamed so loud you'd have thought there'd been a murder.

"It's just me, LaRue," Vern laughed. "What are you doing out here? I've been looking all over for you."

"Vern, don't do that to me! You'll give me a heart attack."

Vern slowly climbed the clubhouse stairs, crawled into the small room, and sat down next to me. He didn't say a word for a long time.

"Come on back in the house, LaRue. Let's go to bed."

I didn't answer.

"Look, honey, I know I've been on edge and not very supportive the last few weeks. . . . I've had one serious confession after another to deal with in the ward and I've been under a lot of pressure at work too. Then there's Michael's mission and Jenny's wedding. Feels like it's just too much and I can't do it all and then you want to go back to school on top of all that."

Better wait a spell till I tell him about the baby, I thought.

"Finishing my degree is real important to me, Vern," I answered. "It's all right with me if you don't understand right now."

Vern was quiet for a long time.

"I love you, LaRue."

Vern's words melted my insides like butter on the stove. Sitting there in the darkness, it kinda dawned on me, right at that moment, that I'd never really understand what Vern was going through most the time and I couldn't really expect him to always understand what I was going through either. Sometimes even lovers could be strangers to each other. We were pretty much left to figure out most stuff by ourselves. But we could watch out for each other—move ahead in the same general direction—keep needing each other.

"I love you too," I answered, taking Vern's hand.

The night wind made the clubhouse sway and creek. The neighbor's dog finally stopped barking. We just sat next to each other in the clubhouse without talking for a long time, but the quiet didn't seem lonesome or tense any more.

"Vern . . . know that talk you gave to the ward a few weeks ago . . . the one where you spoke about people accepting opportunities for service even when they felt they were too busy and that God would bless them? You said something about how a loaded train seldom jumps the tracks?"

"Yeah."

"Think you could handle one more passenger?"

"What do you mean, LaRue?"

"One more passenger . . ."

"LaRue?"

"I had a pregnancy test today."

"You're kidding, right?"

"No."

"Well?"

"I'm pregnant."

Vern's jaw dropped open and he just sat there perfectly still for what seemed an eternity. Then he reached over and cupped my face in both of his palms.

"You sure?"

"Yeah."

“Wow. . . . How far?”

“Due in May.”

“That means we’ll . . . be . . . forty-five when the baby’s born.”

I started crying. Vern drew my face to his shoulder and hugged me real tight.

“Oh, we can do it, honey. Now Christian won’t have to grow up alone. We can do it. You and me together, we can do anything.”

“I’ll have to start wearing those darn granny glasses,” I answered, “or I won’t be able to find the baby.”

Vern chuckled. “I’ll probably have to play catch in the backyard in a wheelchair with an oxygen tank.”

Then Vern crawled into the sleeping bag with me. After trying one position then another, we both finally settled in like two spoons in a drawer. When we touched it felt as if all the tension and distance between us dissolved.

“I can’t believe it, LaRue,” Vern whispered. “Next week we have a missionary farewell, a wedding, and we just found out we’re going to have another baby. I can’t believe it. I feel pretty darn humble about all this.”

“Me too.”

“We’ll have to hang together on this one,” Vern whispered, kissing the back of my neck. “You know, LaRue, we thought we were all through having children before we found out Katie then Christian were on their way too. And now I don’t know how I could get through life without them. I think people stop having babies way too soon these days. You almost have to get as old as we are before you realize what a miracle and a privilege it is to have a child.”

I felt our lives melting together until I couldn’t tell where Vern left off and I began. Just as Vern totally relaxed with his arms around me, I heard a rise in the wind outside and felt a wave of warmth all around and through me.

"Vern . . ." I said, overflowing with a zillion things to say. "Do you think I should quit school now?"

Vern didn't answer right away.

"That's up to you," he finally yawned.

"I'm not going to," I said. "I'm really going to need your help now."

"You've got it," Vern answered.

Chapter Seven

THE NEXT MORNING I WAS MORE than a little stiff. Clubhouses were definitely not designed for middle-aged people with back problems. I slopped around the house in my fuzzy pink slippers trying to read my statistics book on top of an armful of dirty laundry. My head was spinning. I felt like throwing up and passing out at the same time. Nausea and statistic formulas did not mix well. I was taking a big test later that week and I could feel the pressure building.

"Dirty clothes," I mumbled. "Where do all these dirty clothes come from? I could drop dead under a pile of dirty laundry and nobody would notice until they ran out of clean underwear. And look at this house. You'd think a tornado hit. I don't know why I thought I could go to school and keep up with things around here."

I spied all the children swarming around in the kitchen trying to find something to eat. I set my statistics book down on the counter and threw the dirty laundry downstairs in one giant heap.

Walking up to the dining room with my hands on my hips, I spouted, "All right, you guys, listen up. Who's been smooching their greasy little noses and lips all over the windows? And don't say, 'Not me.' And while we're at it, I'd like to know who's been spitting toothpaste on the bathroom mirror, cramming marbles in the heat vents, and using my nice glasses for their model-car paint? And another thing, when you spill a glass of milk or crack an egg in the refrigerator, try to remember someone invented a wash rag hundreds of years ago just for such occasions," I said, trying to balance my reading glasses on top of my head.

"I'd also like to know who left their candy in the hall closet to attract ants and who dug the hole in the backyard I fell in yesterday. And by the way, I never gave my permission to have more baby bunnies around here, so who gave Scamper and Renaldo another honeymoon? Just for your information, I'm not going to catch the chickens when they get loose anymore, and if you want your gym clothes washed, try tossing them in the hamper.

"And another thing, I'm tired of sticky kitchen floors and I've had it up to here with muddy footprints. I will not tolerate any more snails in the bathtub even if they have names. And one more thing. I don't want anyone carrying off my toenail clippers or deodorant any more. And don't think I won't know when you borrow my toothbrush because I can tell 'cause it's still wet."

"Yo, Mom," Michael interrupted with a piece of toast hanging from his mouth. "Chill."

"I have a midterm coming up and I can't figure this stuff out. I'm going to flunk," I answered. "Can't you guys help out a little more around here? Why do you all have to keep eating all the time and wearing clothes?"

No one seemed to be listening. Jennifer was shuffling through the last of her returned wedding invitations with one hand and eating a bagel with the other. Aaron kept pushing eggs around his plate and mashing his toast with his thumb. He had a chess tournament that day during the lunch hour. I think he was practicing his moves on the board. If he won the tournament, he'd get ten bucks and his name on a plaque that would hang in the main hall. Emily was reading a scientific journal and taking notes on index cards for another research paper. Amber was spraying her latest pencil drawing while she made calls to the girls in her Laurel class. Ben was using his butter knife like a musical instrument. He had a clarinet solo in his band concert that evening and was practicing the fingering. Katie crawled across the table to grab the salt shaker. She was supposed to bring a science experiment to school that morning but she forgot. Guess she decided to create a two-second salt crystal. Alisa never actually ate her food, she created miniature villages with it. Everybody, everywhere was always telling her to hurry up, but her one goal in life was to find somewhere to relax so she could settle in with a nice soft blanket and suck on her thumb.

I sighed. It occurred to me that my children's lives were as stressful to them as my life felt to me and I wasn't the only one who needed a little help and support. I needed to quit feeling sorry for myself, stop complaining, and rally the troops.

"Hey kids, good luck with everything today," I said, trying to sound more pleasant. "Go Awesome Willeys! And remember . . . if you keep both feet on the ground, you can't get your pants on!"

All the children turned at exactly the same moment and stared at me. I didn't realize till that moment how grouchy I'd been the past few weeks.

"Sorry about the bad attitude," I said. "It's not your fault."

I noticed relaxed smiles inching their way up my children's faces. Vern walked into the kitchen tying his tie, looking for something to eat.

"Do you think we ought to tell the kids about the

new addition to the family?" I whispered in Vern's ear as he finished positioning his tie and slipped two pieces of bread in the toaster.

"Tonight at family council," Vern whispered back.

Later that night as I sat in the chair watching Vern try to assemble our children, I tried to stifle a chuckle. Vern, who always had such control with his employees down at the bank or ward members down at church, looked like a general surrounded by an inebriated, mutinous crew when he was home with his own children.

As I watched Vern and the kids it occurred to me that there are times when a Willey family council might be compared to a funeral in the sense that you have an uncomfortable gathering of family members who would rather be somewhere else. The major difference was that at a funeral someone has died. At our more trying Willey family councils, someone didn't die but Vern's sense of humor sure did.

"You kids sit up and pay attention," Vern said in a tense, loud voice. "Your mother and I have something important we want to tell you."

Michael, Ben, and Aaron remained tangled in a knot like Sumo wrestlers on the floor. Amber continued sketching a pencil drawing. Emily was reading the sports page while Jenny picked up the phone to call the wedding photographer. Alisa and Katie banged away on the piano singing "Book of Mormon Stories" off key while Christian crawled between their feet sucking on their toes.

Vern glanced over at me and shook his head. "We'll start with our planning calendar," Vern continued, trying not to react to his totally inattentive audience.

Determined to save the day, I marched over to the huge calendar taped to the refrigerator, cleared my throat, then yelled so loud even the neighbors could hear, "Anybody who listens, gets candy."

Then I reached into my pockets and rattled cellophane. Suddenly every child's eyes were on me. Vern looked impressed.

"I've got interviews later tonight, visits on Wednesday, and a stake meeting on Thursday," Vern said, stunned at the sudden undivided attention of our children. I wrote on the weekly calendar taped to the refrigerator. "Oh, and a sealing in the Provo temple on Saturday. Oh, there's a joint activity on Friday with the Scouts and the Young Women. And, of course, Sunday's a goner."

"I've got classes every morning this week, and I'll be working Wednesday, Thursday, and Saturday," Emily added.

Michael and Amber yelled out their work schedules in duet, while Ben and Aaron interrupted with their band and chorus concerts' dates and times. Alisa quietly whispered that she had a school program and parent teacher conferences.

Finally, Katie blurted, "On Wednesday put Katie has to do . . . nothing."

When seven-year-old Katie got something on her mind, I knew it was easier to do what she said than to pay the consequences. So instead of reasoning with her about the silliness of taking up limited calendar space, I quickly wrote exactly what Katie said in the square marked Wednesday.

"On Thursday write, Katie has to . . . goof off," she continued.

I carefully followed my daughter's instructions while the rest of the children giggled. Katie, dressed in her bright orange turtleneck sweater and a delicate pink tutu suddenly realized she had everyone's attention so she decided to perform an impromptu ballet of Swan Lake. Ben moaned about needing time for his homework and Aaron wouldn't quit throwing couch pillows at Michael.

"Kids, your mom and I found out something important yesterday and we want you to be the first to know," Vern announced.

"We're finally getting a Ford truck?" Ben interrupted.

"I'd rather get a horse," Aaron added.

"Can we have one of Olsons' baby goats?" Katie asked.

"No, we're not getting a new van or a horse or a goat," Vern said. "We're getting a new baby."

Suddenly the front room became completely silent.

"Is it a boy or a girl?" Aaron finally broke in.

"Probably," Vern answered.

"Are you sure?" Jenny asked, sounding baffled.

"You guys are too old to be having babies," Emily piped in, obviously taken aback by the news. "What are you thinking? Don't you know about the risk of genetic defects when you get pregnant at your age?" Then she huffed out of the room.

"Hey! Yea! Maybe it'll be a girl," Katie yelled, oblivious to her older sister's fears.

"When's it due?" Amber asked.

"The baby is due in May," Vern answered.

"It's OK, Mommy," Katie said, wrapping her arms around my neck. "The baby can sleep with me."

"Is Mom going to die or something 'cause she's so old?" Michael asked.

"No, your mom's not going to die. But she's going to need your help."

"You can count on me, Mom," Aaron interrupted.

"Yeah, me too," Ben added.

“Me too,” Jenny said, momentarily looking up from her bridal portrait proofs.

“Me too,” Alisa whispered, covering her eyes with her hands and giggling.

“Me too,” Michael said, banging out a beat with the couch pillows on his brother’s head.

“Me too,” Katie added, pulling a flower from her hair.

“Me too,” Amber added.

“Me too,” Christian mimicked.

“Me too,” Vern finished, his voice subdued.

I looked at my whole crazy family and suddenly envisioned my future, the room filled with dozens of grandchildren and great-grandchildren. I’d never run out of babies, thank goodness. I needed to blow my nose but I couldn’t find a tissue, so I sniffed, hard. Just looking at that front room filled with my own private me-tooers made me feel like I could conquer the world, maybe even the universe and beyond . . . right after I took a nap.

Chapter Eight

AN HOUR BEFORE GOING TO CHURCH on the day of Michael's missionary farewell, I walked into Amber's bedroom and found her sitting on the edge of her double bed in a mighty emotional state. Only a year apart in school, Amber and Michael had always been really close.

"Amber, what's the matter?" I asked as if I didn't already know.

"Mom," Amber answered, wiping her eyes. "I've spent every day of my whole life with Michael and now he's leaving me. He's my best friend. I don't know what to do. I won't have anybody to dance with me when nobody else will ask me. Michael can tell what I'm thinking or how I'm feeling just by looking at me. I don't know what to do."

I put my arm around her. "Me either," I said. We sat there on the bed with our arms around each other for a long time. "If we don't stop bawling, our mascara will run and we'll look like scarecrows for our talks today," I said, trying to distract both of us.

Amber almost laughed. "I miss him already and he hasn't even gone yet."

"Me too," I said.

I really didn't think mothers should be required to speak at their sons' missionary farewells. You spent all those years changing his diapers, rocking him to sleep, waving to him on the bus, talking into the wee hours of the night, making sure he ate properly, kissing him on the cheek every night—then all of a sudden you were supposed to throw him into the world with nothing between him and the bad guys but a white shirt and tie and a name tag that read "Elder Willey."

Michael was willing to take all the money he'd earned and saved his *whole* life delivering newspapers and bagging groceries down at Macey's and use it to support himself while he traveled halfway round the world sharing with the German people his love for Jesus and God's plan for their happiness. Most guys his age spent their hard-earned money on cars, college, or girls.

I thought I was ready to see him go. But when the time really came, I wasn't. Two years was a long time. He wouldn't be home to see the new baby born. He wouldn't be home for Christmas or when he turned twenty. He wouldn't be around to turn his stereo up so loud it shook my bedroom floor beams. He wouldn't be around to keep fresh milk on the endangered species list in our refrigerator. He wouldn't be home, at all, for two years.

Later while I sat up on the stand at church, I looked down into the sea of faces in the congregation. I suddenly got this panicked feeling that I'd forgotten to teach Michael something really important but I couldn't remember what it was. Then I noticed several young girls in the audience looking up at my son the same way I looked up at Vern during his farewell twenty-six years before. Kinda made me face the fact that time was passing and I wasn't getting any younger or better-looking.

As I glanced over at Michael, all dressed up in his new missionary suit, white shirt, and tie, I really wanted him to have the growing experience a mission would bring. On the other hand, I also knew that growth would only come from being rejected, from learning to love people who didn't love him back, from serving people who didn't appreciate him, from long days and nights of praying and fasting, from having his heart break. If I hadn't absolutely known that God would step in and make Michael a new heart—bigger and better than the old one—I couldn't have let him go.

Waiting to speak while I sat up on the stand during Michael's missionary farewell felt like the time I waited up all night waiting for him to get born. I kept asking the nurses at the hospital to let me go home. Told them I wasn't *really* in labor, I was just teasing. Sometimes you know in your head that something is happening but in your heart you don't want to feel all the pain just yet.

Somehow I managed to get through my talk, Vern's talk, Michael's talk, and the family musical number, but just barely. I was living proof that giving someone life and giving someone wings . . . hurts. But with all that holding on and letting go, I had come to find a love inside me that never lets go. Nobody had ever told me that being a mother would be so hard and so sweet.

Jenny's wedding was on the Friday following Michael's farewell. My firstborn, Jennifer Willey, and my new son, Richard Moon, were sealed in the Manti Temple at 11:30 on a bright and perfect autumn day. I found myself wishing Jenny and Michael had scheduled these major, life-altering events a little farther apart so that my heart could catch up with my head. Seemed like life was always pushing me over the edge before I was ready to jump.

While I was in the bride's room of the temple helping Jenny get her wedding dress and temple clothing on, sunlight from the window caught the glass chandelier next to the mirrors, flashing rainbows of light all about the small room. As I watched Jenny comb through her hair, all our yesterdays drifted through my mind: the first time I held her in my arms, a tiny premature infant looking up at me with such wonder in her clear blue eyes . . . tucking her in bed at night . . . watching her race like the wind on her first track-and-field day . . . helping with the red roses on her first date.

Then I remembered a day at Salem Pond when Jenny was eleven. As soon as we pulled up next to the water she darted from the car and ran toward the geese she'd spotted. In her eagerness she scared the birds and they flew away.

"Oh, Momma, I scared 'em," Jenny said. "I just want to hold 'em."

"Sometimes," I had answered her, "you have to sit quietly and wait for them to feel safe. Then they come to you."

Jenny sat quietly at the edge of the water and waited. The birds watched her, and in time they approached cautiously. She extended her hand. They stepped back. When she rose they raced back to the water and flew away again.

"They're so beautiful," Jenny said, standing next to me. Then she noticed some young boys on the other side of the pond with BB guns. "What if they hurt them? I could take one home and tend it and feed it and keep it safe."

Jenny stepped away from me toward another group of wild birds lacing their way through the cattails. She slowly knelt and reached out again, but the wild birds swam out of her reach. I watched Jenny follow the animals with her eyes as they stretched their wings and soared away.

"Will you help me catch one?" she asked. "I could take it home and keep it safe."

“It would be safe,” I answered, “but it wouldn’t be free.”

“You’re right, Momma,” Jenny said after a long, thoughtful moment of quiet. “I think wild birds shouldn’t be pets. I can love ’em best here on the shore.”

Now my Jenny was ready to take flight, and I was left to love her best from the shore.

After that quiet moment of remembering as I watched my daughter dress in the bride’s room, it came to me: all my love for Jenny would go on; all those years of caring for her and helping her grow up *mattered*—they mattered more than anything else I could have chosen to do with my life. What greater gift could I give the world than Jennifer Marie Willey—my own personal wonder of the world? Jenny was the best fifth-grade teacher in the history of the universe and beyond. Someday Jenny would have her own baby, and our love would go on—forever.

While I helped Jenny with her veil I felt this intense longing to hold the moment, tuck it away like some rich summer harvest so I could pull it out on a cold winter night. But it was time for the sealing ceremony, then pictures outside the temple, a wedding breakfast, greeting guests, and a reception. I just wanted time to stand still for a moment. But there was no stopping it, not even for a second.

When Jenny was through dressing, she looked at me and smiled. All our years together felt like a leaf in the wind, here one moment and then suddenly gone on the next breeze. People always told me to notice all the firsts . . . the first smile, first tooth, first day in school, first date. Why didn’t anyone tell me to notice the lasts . . . the last time Jenny held my hand on the way to school, the last time she needed help with her buttons, the last time she smiled at me before she stepped from childhood to become someone's wife.

As Jenny turned toward the hall, ready to meet Richard in the sealing room, she no longer needed my hand. But I needed hers. I reached out and grasped her gentle fingertips just for an instant before I let go. Then she was gone. For a minute I couldn't even swallow or breathe.

The rest of the day was a whirl of pictures, flowers, parties, food, and faces. Late that night, long after the sealing ceremony, breakfast, and reception, Vern and I dragged the last sagging section of wedding cake, gift box, and flower arrangement from the van into our house and collapsed on the couch. We were so exhausted we could hardly move.

Later, in our pajamas, after all the other children had gone to bed, we took out the video Uncle Marvin and Aunt Leanne had made for Jenny and Richard using dozens of pictures of their childhood and teenage years. We watched our daughter and new son-in-law, with the aid of computer programming, grow up instantly before our eyes. We just sat there like a couple of dopes bawling.

"When did she grow up?" Vern asked in a hushed voice. "Wasn't I there? Where's the time gone, LaRue? You spend all this time loving them and raising them—so they can just leave?"

"Yeah," I answered.

Now, as if all this marriage and farewell stuff weren't enough, a few days later we had to drop Michael off at the missionary training center in Provo. Michael had spent several days after the wedding going through all the stuff in his bedroom, throwing out old school papers, shorts, T-shirts, and stuffed animals. Then he boxed up the rest, but not before he gave his stereo to Vern and me for safekeeping.

During the morning of the day Michael was to leave, Vern came home early from work and gave our oldest son a father's blessing. I watched my husband with his strong broad hands on Michael's head giving words to his love and asking God to watch over and bless our boy.

After lunch Michael drove around town and picked up all his brothers and sisters at school before we loaded up the van with his luggage and headed for Provo. Vern and Amber tried to joke around on the way over so that we all wouldn't bust up bawling and make it harder on Michael.

The missionary training center was so busy they had traffic control men in little orange vests directing cars where to unload and park. There were over three hundred young men and women entering the center that day and about three thousand missionaries receiving training there already. They ushered our whole family in one door and Michael in another. Then they checked in the luggage. Next Michael, Vern, and I and all the rest of the kids were ushered into a large assembly room, where someone up front talked to us, showed us a film, and led us in a hymn. Then the man in charge told the missionaries to leave through one door and the families through another.

It was almost more than I could stand—one short hug and then you were supposed to just walk through a door and leave? Vern and I and all the other kids braced ourselves against the cold brick wall out in the hall and stretched our necks to see if we could catch one last glimpse of Michael turning the corner to walk away. I'd just read in the newspaper about a missionary in Russia who had been stabbed to death. I'd taught and trained Michael all his life and hoped that he would want to serve a mission. Then when the time came and I had to actually say good-bye, I couldn't even speak.

After dropping Michael off at the MTC and watching Jenny get married, I went home and tried to get on with the business of living without them. But there were two empty places at the table, two children who weren't in bed when I went to check on them in the middle of the night.

Someone had once said to me, "Guess it's not so hard to have your children leave home when you have so many to take their place."

"No one can take a child's place," I had answered. "Each one of my children has all my love. You can't divide up your love like a piece of pie—every child only getting his or her fraction. Every child gets the whole pie."

Nobody really warned me when I had a baby that my job description for the next twenty years included working myself out of a job.

But days grew into weeks and weeks into months, and I learned that life keeps going on. Autumn color melted like honey from the mountains to our valley floor. Ring-necked pheasants hid in our vegetable garden while orange-vested hunters stalked our back acre or took to the hills. All our apples sweetened with the cold snap in the air. Halloween came and went.

The rest of that autumn I spent staying up till two or three in the morning studying—the only time of day I could be sure I wouldn't be interrupted. I was glad for the focus and work my new classes gave me. They kept me from feeling sorry for myself. Sitting in a classroom with the sole purpose of learning something new made me feel right queenly. I didn't have to sweep the classroom floor, wipe off the blackboard, or keep the other students in line. All I had to do was sit there . . . and *learn.*

Sometimes I worried that a large man in an official

uniform would march into the classroom, take me by the arm, and tell me I didn't belong there—that I needed to go home and finish the dishes. I picked the brain of every professor, trying to make sure I learned as much as I could before I was through.

My exercise sessions with Vern were going as well as could be expected, considering the waves of nausea that kept sneaking up on me whenever I least expected them. Riding the bike while Vern jogged alongside was not conventional, but it was plenty to get my heart rate up. I could pedal alongside and sing at the top of my lungs.

Snow fell the night before Thanksgiving. Before sunrise, Alisa and Katie stampeded down the dark hall to my bedroom, blurting, "Mom and Dad, it snowed last night!"

Before I could rub the sleep from my eyes, my little girls raced back down the hall, located their winter clothes, and dashed out the back door into the quiet predawn stillness. I slowly rolled to my side, groaning, propped my body up with my arms, then waited for the blood to make it to my head. I dangled my feet over the bed, then stood and waddled to the bathroom. By the time I made it back to my frosted window pane I could see Katie and Alisa lying on their backs waving their arms and legs up and down in the white snow.

"They'll get snow down their pants and backs and end up with numb bums," I mumbled.

Just then Alisa and Katie carefully stood and jumped away from their impressions in the snow.

Oh . . . snow angels. I'd forgotten.

My children's ability to have good old-fashioned fun seemed to me the purest and most honest expression of gratitude.

"Vern, come look," I said, tapping him on the shoulder in bed.

Vern drowsily rolled over, sat up, walked to the window, and looked out.

"Vern," I whispered, "Look . . . angels."

"The ones in the snow or the ones throwing snowballs at each other?" Vern asked.

"Both," I answered. "Just think, our Father in Heaven trusts us with another one."

"Maybe He's just hard up," Vern answered.

I traced with my finger the intricate lace pattern of frost forming on the window. "Look, Vern. Isn't it beautiful? Just think, if we didn't take the time to notice, all this beauty would be wasted."

Vern put his arm around my shoulder. "I'll start a fire downstairs so it will be warm when the kids come back inside. You can put the pies in the oven."

When the house was warmed with the scent of bumbleberry pies and quick-burning pine, I helped Alisa and Katie out of their wet clothes and into dry flannel dresses and long stockings. Then I French-braided their hair and tied big red bows on the ends.

While I stirred the hot chocolate in a big pot on the stove, I watched my teenage sons in the backyard firing round white cannon bombs at each other behind snow forts they'd constructed from large square blocks of snow.

Like the wave of heat after you open the oven door, I felt suddenly warm inside. I knew that Thanksgiving morning—down deep—that this moment was enough; I had everything. I felt overwhelming gratitude for Vern and each of my children. I knew my family was my greatest work, their happiness and development my strongest, deepest desire.

Then after two months of training in Provo, Michael was scheduled to leave for Germany from the Salt Lake

City airport in early December. Family and friends were allowed to meet missionaries at the airport for one last quick good-bye. As if I needed one more farewell to childhood about now.

Michael looked so shiny that day at the airport—couldn't wipe the smile off his face. He took his time talking to each person in the family and gave us each a hug good-bye. Then he picked up his bags and walked down the long tunnel toward the airplane with his companion.

Right before he turned the last corner to step onto the jet, Michael dropped his carry-on luggage, turned around to get one last look at his family, took a deep breath, and jumped with a whoop—arms and legs spread-eagle in midair. Then he was gone.

The whole family rushed over to the airport terminal window and pressed our greasy noses against the glass as the plane backed up and headed for takeoff. After taxiing down the runway, the airplane soared smoothly into the smoky blue sky. We followed the plane until it was a tiny speck dissolving into the horizon. The whole family stood there a long time, motionless, staring through the glass at the enormous sky, before we slowly accepted the fact that Michael was really gone.

I reached for Vern's hand. There in the blur and chaos of children, grandparents, and strangers bustling all around us, Vern grabbed me and wrapped his arms around me so tight I couldn't breathe.

Standing on my tiptoes so I could reach his cheek to give him a kiss, I whispered, "I'm still here."

We didn't let go of each other for a long time.

I actually managed to survive all my finals during those middle weeks of December. My physical education instructor even let me ride my bicycle for the final cardiovascular endurance test because I was pregnant and jogging might not be good for the baby at my age. When I was through he informed me that I'd improved from *pathetic* to *fair* in my fitness level measurement and would, as such, pass his course. It was perhaps the crowning moment of the semester for me.

I finished up fall semester—much to my shock and everyone else's in the family—with a 4.0 average. Even Emily did a double take when I showed her my report card (now, remember, that girl was pretty darn hard to impress).

Then, on the weekend before Christmas, I started bleeding. When I called the doctor, he told me not to worry but to stay down and he'd schedule an ultrasound for me over at the hospital early Monday morning.

Chapter Nine

"TAKE A DEEP BREATH," VERN SAID, patting me on the back as we turned into the hospital parking lot in Provo for the ultrasound test. He could tell I was a little nervous. "Everything will be all right. You've had some bleeding with several of the other babies and everything turned out all right."

Vern was always calm and reassuring. He was also the kind who never peeked at his Christmas presents early. Said it ruins the surprise. I was a box rattler from the word go. So we had different views about wanting to find out the sex of the baby with this ultrasound test. Vern would be content to wait till I delivered to find out if we were the proud parents of a new daughter or son. Me, on the other hand, I could hardly wait to find out. I thought ultrasounds were the best invention since indoor plumbing. I loved calling my baby by name while I rubbed my tummy for months before I delivered.

The prenatal department was down a long hall to our right on the third floor. Several pregnant ladies were waiting in one room and several others were waddling down the hall when Vern and I walked up to the information window. A nurse directed both of us to a small, dark room filled with technical-looking machinery. In the center of the room was a raised examination table next to a large machine with a screen or monitor. The nurse asked me to step up on the table and lie down. Then she exposed my tummy and draped me with white towels.

"The prenatologist will be here in a few minutes," the nurse said. "You can roll on your side if you get uncomfortable waiting on your back. Would you like a video tape of the test?"

"Love one," I answered.

"Just pay the girl at the window two dollars and I'll let you have one of these." Then she placed an empty black cassette near the machine at my right.

Vern was quiet. He sat in a chair looking like he might fall asleep. If you turned out the lights and let Vern sit down for more than two minutes, he'd be a goner. I found a television screen placed strategically above our heads straight in front of us.

"Look," I said. "Bet that's where we look."

Vern was quiet. I fidgeted around trying to get comfortable. Felt like a child on Christmas morning. When the prenatologist finally walked through the door, I rolled onto my back and sighed, "Boy, I'm glad you're here. I hope you can tell me if our baby's all right. Been having some bleeding."

The doctor exposed my tummy, then squeezed a gel-like substance over my belly and began rubbing an instrument across my abdomen.

"To start," the doctor said, "I'm just going to get a few measurements. . . . There's the head."

I saw the image of my unborn child suddenly appear in fuzzy black and white on the television screen overhead. There were the tiny features, the eyes, the ears, the nose, and mouth.

"Oh, Vern, look."

Vern was quiet.

"Those are the hands up next to the face," the doctor

continued. "Seems like all babies I see like to have their hands up next to their face."

I watched as the doctor took several more measurements of the head then moved down to take a measurement of the femur bone in the leg.

"It looks like you better move that due date up a week or so," the doctor continued. "Do you two want to know if it's a girl or a boy?"

"Yes."

"See, right there," the doctor said, pointing with a star image on the screen. "Looks like a little girl to me."

"A girl?" Vern answered. "Whew . . . won't have to go through Cub Scouts again."

"Because of your age," the doctor interrupted, "you have a greater chance of having a baby with genetic defects. The ultrasound image can tell us only so much. We can tell much more with a few tests your obstetrician has ordered. We'll have those results for you as soon as possible." I reached for Vern's hand and felt his firm grip. "Then you can decide if you want to have an abortion or not at that point," the doctor continued.

"No," Vern said.

"Abortion's not an option for us," I added.

"Don't be so sure. You have to consider the quality of life, yours and the child's."

"Whatever condition our baby is in, she's our daughter and we'll take care of her," Vern said all peaceful like and full of quiet strength.

As I listened to Vern and felt his strong hand wrapped around mine, it suddenly dawned on me that I had the romance I'd been longing for all along. Real love—real romance—was facing whatever life threw your way—together. I didn't have to wait for the Publishers Sweepstakes people to come to my door for my life to be exciting. I only had to wake up and pay attention to the life I already had. There in that darkened room of the hospital with Vern at my side, I understood that accepting the ordinariness, challenges, and hard work of life together—however they were given us—was as romantic and daring as it gets.

When all the procedures were finished, Vern and I silently walked to the car in the parking lot.

"Know that night my Dad died?" Vern asked, quietly breaking the silence. "They had him hooked up to all those machines measuring his breathing and pulse and everything? I was sitting there next to him in a chair holding his hand—watching all those instrument readings get lower and lower and slower and slower—and my mind flashed back to the times when I was sitting by you when our babies were born, except your readings kept getting faster and faster and higher and higher.

"I knew watching Dad leave that dying and being born aren't so different. Going and coming from this earth, there's no easy way in or out. It's reverent, sacred."

"Know what you mean, Vern," I answered.

Several weeks later, I received a phone call from Doc Dillard. I immediately sensed something was seriously wrong.

"LaRue?" Doc Dillard said. "I have the results of your ultrasound and the follow-up on your genetic tests. I'd like you and your husband to come to my office as soon as possible and talk to me about the results. I'll have the prenatologist who performed the tests here to answer any questions."

"Why, is something wrong?" I asked.

"I'd rather not say until I have both you and your husband, together. It would be better for both of you that way I think."

I couldn't think of what to say. "When?" I finally asked. "When do you want us to come in?"

"How about tomorrow at ten?"

"We'll be there."

That twenty-four-hour wait for the appointment was torture.

"Vern and LaRue," Doc Dillard said after he'd invited us into his office, "please take a seat and make yourselves comfortable."

After he introduced us to Doctor Clark, the doctor who had performed the ultrasound, I glanced up nervously at Doc Dillard behind the desk shuffling some papers in his hands.

"I'll have Doctor Clark fill you in on the results of the tests we've run," Doc Dillard said, glancing to his colleague.

"I'm very sorry I have to give you such grim news today," Doctor Clark said. "After all the tests we've run, we have reason to believe you are carrying a female fetus with Edwards syndrome, a disease that causes mental retardation, disfiguration, and sometimes early death. You also have partial placenta previa, which means that some of the placenta has implanted over the cervix. That's what's causing your bleeding. If you don't go to bed, you will continue bleeding, and probably deliver early, and the baby will die. All things considered, that may be a blessing. Or we could perform an abortion as soon as possible."

I remember that Doctor Clark's voice suddenly seemed to be echoing through a long tunnel and the room began spinning. I felt a numbness in my arms and legs. I quickly took Vern's hand and held it until both our knuckles went white.

"What are you saying?" I asked, shaking my head

trying to understand. "If I don't go to bed now, our daughter will be born too early and die and that will be a blessing? Or I can have an abortion? What kind of a choice is that?"

"You haven't seen children with Edwards syndrome. I can assure you. It would be a blessing," Doctor Clark answered.

I was quiet for a long time. Nobody said anything. Vern and I were trying to sort through it, I guess.

"This is our daughter you're talking about, not the results of some test," I finally answered, breaking the long silence. "Labs can make mistakes."

"Doesn't matter what shape she's in," Vern added. "We'll take care of her."

The prenatologist shook his head and turned to Doc Dillard for support.

"LaRue and Vern, you already have nine children," Doc Dillard added half-heartedly, trying to lend support to his colleague. "Maybe it would be a blessing. At least think about it. Even if you think having a handicapped child won't be hard on you two, think about your other children."

"Why would we kill our own daughter just because her body or her mind is less than perfect?" I asked.

"We have a home with mentally handicapped boys in our ward," Vern added. "Those boys teach us how to slow down, how to give without expecting something in return, how to love. If our baby has problems, she's still our baby. She deserves all the love and kindness we have to offer."

"Well, that sounds courageous, but you really don't understand what you will be getting into," Doctor Clark answered. "The day after day pressure of caring for a deformed and retarded child takes a terrible toll. At least promise me to think about it for a few days before you make a final decision. Consider everything, especially the strain on your marriage."

"We don't need a few days to think about it," Vern and I chorused together like we had planned it out or something.

Both doctors grew quiet. I guess they finally understood Vern and I meant what we said. We had considered this possibility privately and together when we found out about this pregnancy. We'd talked about it many times through the years with our other pregnancies. We both understood we could have a sick, deformed, or retarded child every time we got pregnant. But we were willing to take that risk.

Now that chance had become a reality. We knew without thinking what we would do. We didn't feel heroic or anything. We didn't need time to think about it. Abortion wasn't an option. Encouraging an early delivery so the baby would die wasn't an option.

"No couple who decides to bring a baby into this world knows what kind of hand they're going to get dealt," I said, looking Doc Dillard in the eye. "Just 'cause medicine is so fancy we can find out something's wrong before our babies are born, doesn't give us the right to kill our own children without giving them a fighting chance. If you won't support our decision, we'll find a doctor who will."

"You don't have to find another doctor," Doc Dillard answered quickly.

Then Vern and I stood to leave. Both doctors shook our hands in silence.

After we left the doctor's office and walked toward the car in the parking lot, Vern turned to me, hitched up his pants, and stated, "LaRue, I'm going to take you home and put you right to bed. And don't worry about your school classes. I'll figure out a way so you won't have to quit, LaRue. I promise."

I was speechless, if you can believe it.

"I know how busy you are, Vern," I finally said. "You don't have any time to waste . . ."

"I don't have any time to waste," Vern answered real slow like, "on things that don't matter as much as you. LaRue, you matter more than anything in this world to me."

Chapter Ten

VERN AND I DECIDED AFTER SEVERAL days of praying and fasting that we wouldn't tell the children or anyone else about the problems with the baby. We'd cross that bridge when we came to it. We didn't want to get caught in the swirl of other people's opinions about what we should do. But late at night in bed together, we would talk about our unborn daughter and hold each other real close until we fell asleep.

Winter semester started on the first week of January, and Vern sure did keep his word. While I was one big, lazy body in bed getting fatter by the minute, Vern found a student in each of my classes willing to videotape each lecture. Emily was up on campus during the day so she could drive my assignments, papers, and lecture videos back and forth from our home to campus. Vern monitored me while I took my tests, so he could sign a paper verifying I didn't cheat. He organized the older children and ward members to help tend Christian and fix meals. He took on the laundry as a personal challenge. Though we all wore pink underwear, nobody complained.

While I was in bed, I found that people tend to visit more often when they know exactly where they can find you. Brother Lamb built me a free-standing lap desk so I could keep up with reading and writing for my classes in bed. Sister Valdez from the ward brought me a box full of all kinds of exotic herbs guaranteed to fix whatever was ailing me. The boys from Maeser house brought me original paintings to hang on my bedroom walls and keep me happy. Earnest Wilson read me poetry by Emerson, Whitman, Longfellow, and Thoreau.

Even Delbert Mendenhall showed up at my bedside on a regular basis. Once, after more than an hour of mostly nonverbal communication and sheet tapping, Delbert ordered his wife from the bedroom then finally blurted, "Sister Bishop? I believe Jesus now. Just thought you'd like to know."

I took Delbert's hand to his total embarrassment.

"I know, Delbert. I can see it in your eyes."

"But I'm blind."

"Not any more Delbert. You see pretty good now."

"Thanks for visitin' me," Delbert said. "Know I was awful. Shoulda apologized a long time ago."

Delbert's wife stuck her head around the corner, caught my eye, and winked.

"Don't have to apologize or thank me," I answered. "You're my friend."

Then Delbert did something I'll never forget. He slowly brought my hand up to his cheek then kissed me softly on the knuckles like I was a queen or something.

"You're the best friend I ever had," Delbert whispered.

Right before Delbert left that night, Sister Mendenhall softly whispered in my ear, "You saved my husband. He was so low after his suicide attempt failed. I just knew he'd try again. Then you started coming to visit. I'll never be able to thank you enough."

Sometimes you have no idea that the little annoying things you do will eventually make a difference in someone's life. Because of the Mendenhalls I'll never feel that way again.

During those long weeks in bed all that winter, I thought a lot about the baby growing inside me. I wondered what my life would be like caring for a child with severe mental and physical handicaps. I wondered how all the changes she would bring would affect her brothers and sisters and if I had the patience and energy to cope with a child who would never grow up. I wondered how people in the ward would react, if strangers in the grocery store would stare. I wondered if I should have followed my doctor's advice years ago and quit having babies at my age. I wondered about pretty much everything at one time or another, but I never doubted I should do everything in my power to give this child a chance to live.

Studying hard for my classes helped me focus my attention on other things, but I still had a lot of time left over for thinking. I prayed more than I'd ever prayed before, not for God to take away this challenge, but for the strength to cope with the new demands this child would bring. During those long cold months, I believe I learned more from watching the cherry tree outside my bedroom window than all my classes put together. Day after day, during those long months in bed, I watched the black limbs of the tree face the canyon wind, a hundred days of cold and snow. Week after week, month after month, alone in the freezing wind, that huge tree bent but never broke.

It came to me one day where that tree got its strength. Huge roots buried deep in the earth held that cherry tree to life day after day, night after night. So I searched for my own roots. Gradually, after the humble moments of silent pleading that grew into hours, days, and months, I felt re-created inside. One fine morning as predawn sunlight filtered in through my bedroom window, I gave God the only gift I had to offer, all my heart's longing to do His will. That morning was for me the defining moment of my life.

I glanced out the window and noticed something new appearing on the smallest limbs of the cherry tree. Like kernels of popcorn, cherry blossoms had burst during the night—their honey sweet scent drifted through my opened window. I felt something bursting inside myself—a soft, quiet, thankful feeling followed by a gentle joy I cannot describe. I knew at that moment, our unborn daughter's name should be Joy.

I realized that most of my life I'd been so blessed with all the good stuff, like health, people to love, and something useful to do. But I hadn't even noticed or felt grateful for it. Scrubbing a floor, fixing a meal, or throwing in a batch of laundry suddenly seemed like privileges instead of drudgery. I felt truly awake for the first time to the richness of my life, cherry blossoms, sunshine, laughter. Every day seemed a gift.

And my children talked to me a lot more while I was in bed, probably because I wasn't rushing around the house or charging off to another meeting all the time. I had more time to look into their eyes and be touched by what I saw looking back at me. I came to understand that God had led me to the opening of a great diamond mine and said, "LaRue, you can have as many diamonds as you want before your time runs out." I knew my children were literally my mother-load, my jewels.

One night Emily, still deciding what to do with her life, came into my bedroom and sat on the side of the bed next to me.

"If I ever get married," Emily said after she'd filled me in on her plans to work on an archaeology dig in Jordan that summer and attend Harvard next fall, "I don't want to give up being me. Nothing personal, Mom, but don't you ever wonder what your life would have been like if you'd had a career, maybe gone to New York and become a famous writer or something?"

"I heard this story about a famous author once," I answered. "When he was on his deathbed, surrounded by all his prestigious awards and books, his agent asked him if he was content. The author told his agent if he had it to do over again, each one of those books or awards would be a grandchild. Emmy, to me a career is what you do to sustain life but it's not a life. Life to me, Em, is people—people I love. If I had to choose between New York or giving you life, I'd take you every time."

"Oh, Mom, be perfectly honest. Don't you ever wonder what you could have become? Don't you ever regret giving your life away for Dad and us kids?"

"I haven't given up my life, Em—I've found it. I just feel grateful. I know that's hard to understand right now, but it's true. All these college classes I've been taking, they're so interesting and fine—love learning. But I realize now I've been getting the best education all along, all through these years. Raising a family, loving, washing, cleaning—all that stuff—it's changed me, made me different. I feel so much more love."

"Yeah, you have lots of people who love you."

"I mean I have so many people I love, Emmy," I answered. "I'm not saying raising a family is more important than your personal development. I want you to get your doctor's degree. I'm real proud of you. I'm just saying being home day after day, lovin' and takin' care of you and your brothers and sisters and sharing it all with your Dad, it's changed me inside, made me better . . . maybe more than a Ph.D. . . . maybe more than being famous. My life with Dad and you children . . . it's real, Em. You all rescued me from myself. You're the best thing I've ever done. When I die, all that matters is who I am inside, not how much stuff I have or how many people know my name. You, Emily Jean Willey, you are my masterpiece."

Emily smiled. I knew it would be years until she truly understood.

I was able to keep up with my classes because a whole army of people stepped up to the line and went to work . . . for me. Part of the best education I received all those long months in bed was a lesson in how many people loved me back. Watching Vern and all the kids, neighbors, and ward members work their tails off to help me graduate made me feel so grateful, like it would take a lifetime to pay everybody back. The kids even kept their rooms clean, and if that's not a miracle I don't know what is.

Brother Wilson from the ward brought over his laptop computer. Sister Grayson and Sister Ainge brought over boxes of canned peaches and pears. The boys from Maeser house kept my walls filled with new crayon and watercolor masterpieces, and they sang Primary songs to me whenever they came to visit.

"'I am a child of God, and he has sent me here,'" John sang in his best monotone on one of my favorite visits.

After finishing his song, he said, "Sister Bishop, your tummy's getting fat." He proudly rubbed his own protruding stomach. "Maybe I'm gonna have a baby too." Then he reached over and patted my face. "I love you, Sister Bishop," he said.

"I love you too, John," I answered, wrapping my arms around him.

Once when Sister Bell was over proofreading my final

research paper, she stopped suddenly with her corrections on my grammar, took a deep breath, and sighed, "I wish I'd had the courage to keep having children like you, LaRue."

Her comment caught me off guard. I knew Melva Dawn Bell had raised three responsible, successful children who lived in major cities across the country.

"I was older when I got married. After I had our three children, I started reading all the latest studies about the risk of genetic problems increasing as women aged. I thought I'd better quit while I was ahead if you know what I mean, not tempt fate. And I wanted to go back to work."

I tried to say something to comfort Melva but she brushed off my comments and went on.

"I just knew I couldn't handle it if I had a less than perfect child. I was scared to death I'd have a Down's syndrome baby or something like that and people would stare. I just couldn't take the chance. I regret that decision about as much as anything I've ever done. Now I have Parkinson's and people stare at me all the time because my arms shake and my head bobs and they think I'm retarded. I know my mind is slowly deteriorating—my brain cells are dying. I know that because of this disease, someday someone will probably have to take care of me—maybe even change my diapers and feed me. But I'll always be me inside. And I know I'll just want to feel loved—to be needed—to feel useful. I understand now that a person can be useful even if all they're able to do is help others learn to serve and love because they're unable to take care of themselves. I realize now that all life is sacred. I've learned that through personal experience, LaRue. I've learned the hard way."

That was the first time I'd ever seen Sister Bell get

emotional. At that moment I realized God had been trying to get a message through to me but I'd been too distracted to listen. So He'd sent His message through Melva Dawn Bell.

I sure did enjoy every minute of my studies winter semester. My classes were all downright fascinating in their own way. It seemed like a miracle to sit and read hour after hour. Found I didn't want to watch television or even listen to music much. The quiet time for reading and thinking seemed almost religious, as if I was feeding my soul.

I finished my last final exam at exactly 11:37 P.M. on April 19. Vern and all the kids stayed up late and waited in the front room playing Rook and throwing popcorn. When I whistled from the bedroom and told them I was finished, I'd never seen such a celebration. Ben threw confetti all over the bedroom while Aaron tooted on the bull horn. Even Emily hugged me so tight I couldn't breath for a minute. Vern danced around the room with Alisa and Katie on each foot and Amber unrolled a butcher paper sign that read, "You Did It, Mom!"

"*We* did it," I said, grinning from ear to ear. "Thanks guys."

Chapter Eleven

BYU GRADUATION WAS ON THE brilliant, clear spring morning on April 23. The lilacs were in bloom and the daffodils and tulips were up all over town, shouting for everybody to wake up and start living. I had three weeks to go before my due date so Doc Dillard advised me to stay in bed. Vern ordered me a cap and gown anyway. He videotaped the grand graduation procession that morning in the Marriott center and all the fine speeches and everything so I could watch it later.

At my college convocation that afternoon, Vern walked across the stage in the de Jong Concert Hall and received my diploma. He put a pillow under his shirt so he could look more like me. Jennifer's new husband videotaped that part. When Vern and the kids got home, about a hundred people from the ward came over and we ate sloppy joes and cookies and ice-cream like it was going out of style. Then we watched my graduation, with Vern as my stand in, on the television.

Toward evening Vern helped me slip on my cap and gown, then carefully set the timer on the camera, jumped in bed next to me, and snapped our picture. Looked pretty funny with my huge belly draped in black graduation robes trying to balance my cap while I was all wrapped up in Vern. We were laughing so hard Vern thought I was teasing him when I suddenly held still and gasped.

"Vern, maybe you shouldn't have jumped on the bed so hard," I said. "My water just broke."

"Sure," Vern laughed.

Then Vern looked at me, and in a second he could tell I wasn't teasing. He knew from past experience that I didn't take much time having babies so he sprang into action pronto.

"We're having a baby!" Vern yelled down the hall from our bedroom with his hands cupped around his mouth. The whole house suddenly grew quiet. "Gang way. We're coming through."

Vern grabbed me a towel from the bathroom, hurried over to the bed, and lifted me gently into his arms. "Hold on to my neck, LaRue," Vern whispered. "I'll get you there, honey."

The ride over to the hospital was pretty quiet. Vern and I held hands real tight.

"You havin' contractions?" Vern asked, trying not to speed.

"Yeah," I answered, trying not to scare him too much and cause an accident.

"I love you, LaRue," Vern said softly as we screeched up to the hospital parking lot. "Remember, however things turn out, honey, everything will be all right. We can do this—you and me together."

They had a wheelchair at the hospital emergency entrance and took us immediately upstairs to the obstetrics ward. When the nurse called Doc Dillard he told her we were expecting a daughter with severe mental and physical handicaps, so she also called in a whole team of newborn specialists. After Doc Dillard got to the hospital, he was pretty quiet. He didn't say anything while he was preparing for delivery. He seemed pretty serious.

"We're ready, LaRue," Doc finally said. "All these

people know how to help you and your baby. Don't hold back. One nice long push here and . . ."

After the swell of pain had reached its peak and I knew our daughter had slipped into the world, I opened my eyes and tried to sit up. Vern brushed my sweaty forehead with the palm of his hand. Then I saw Doc Dillard's face. He had a look in his eyes that was almost reverent.

"LaRue and Vern," Doc Dillard said, "congratulations. You have a beautiful daughter. She looks . . . perfectly normal."

Vern and I looked at each other, stunned. The team of doctors in the room quickly took our daughter down to the newborn intensive care nursery to run some tests, so it was just me and Vern and Doc Dillard in the delivery room for a while.

"She looks beautiful," Doc Dillard said again. "I couldn't see one thing wrong with her. But then I guess you can't always tell by looking."

Vern and I just stared at each other. We didn't have to say anything to know what the other was thinking. Later, after I was wheeled into my hospital room, Vern sat on a chair at the side of my bed, took my hand, and sighed a deep-down total exhaustion sigh.

"We can't find anything wrong with her," the newborn specialist said later when he walked into my room. "Of course we'll have to run more tests and keep a close eye on her but it looks like she's a perfectly normal baby girl."

"I'll call the kids," Vern said, his face beaming and his eyes filled with tears.

"That won't be necessary," the doctor answered. "There's about a hundred people out here in the hall."

I guess lots of people had followed us over from the graduation party 'cause it seemed like everybody and the kitchen sink came into my room to congratulate me and Vern. Then they all raced down to the nursery and watched Joy—that's what we named her—get her first bath.

Later, *all* Joy's tests turned out normal. The lab that made her diagnosis had just made a terrible mistake. Vern and I decided not to tell anyone about the earlier test results and our decision to continue with the pregnancy even after our doctors had advised otherwise. Joy would remain our private miracle.

It wasn't long before we couldn't even remember what life was like without our new daughter. She came into the world smiling, hiccupping, and brought so much love into our home. I can't tell you how glad we were that she came to our family. It's a good thing we're not always in charge of how our lives turn out. God does a much better job.

Going back to school that year sure taught me a lot—just not the things I expected. Learning from books was grand, but it was no substitute for learning from life. I learned real love isn't anything like in the movies—real love, real romance is what me and Vern have. I learned that lovin' people and devoting your life to them is *always* worth it even if those people don't notice, appreciate you, or even love you back—cause lovin' changes me. The pay's not the love you get back, but the love you feel inside. And I learned to trust God—all the time.

Yep, my days were still full of lots of diapers, dishes, and laundry—but it seemed different—like a privilege instead of a life sentence. Vern was still bishop and gone most of the time but I could see how it had changed Vern and me, making us softer inside. Didn't mean I was sporting a halo or something. Still had my bad days and did my fair share of complaining, but mostly I felt peaceful inside—'cause I knew what I was doing was the most important thing in the world.

The first time I took my newborn daughter and little Christian for a walk in the stroller up the road and back, Joy was about three weeks old. I stopped just long enough at the brow of the hill to really look around me at the wide open sky, green fields of new-grown barley and snowcapped mountains. I felt this gentle power deep down inside—like I was connected with the whole universe. At the same time I felt this incredible smallness, this constant hunger for the hand of God.

Then Joy grew restless in the stroller and cried to be held. As I took her in my arms, I silently wondered *what if I'd listened to the doctors instead of my heart? What if . . . I'd chosen anything over love?*

When Joy settled down, I put her back in the stroller and headed for home. I had one fine day ahead of me—washing, cooking, defrosting the freezer, rocking Joy to sleep, reading Christian a story . . .

"Wow, all this and heaven too," I whispered to myself.

About the Author

JANENE WOLSEY BAADSGAARD is often referred to as Mormonism's answer to Erma Bombeck. She has written numerous newspaper columns and features, magazine articles, and books. Some of her books include: *Is There Life After Birth? A Sense of Wonder; Why Does My Mother's Day Potted Plant Always Die? On the Roller Coaster Called Motherhood; Families Who Laugh . . . Last; Family Finances for the Flabbergasted;* and *Grin & Share It: Raising a Family with a Sense of Humor.*

A graduate of Brigham Young University, she has been a *Deseret News* columnist and feature writer and home and family editor for the *Utah County Journal.* She is a frequent contributor to the *New Era* and the *Ensign* magazines and has taught English and literature courses for Utah Valley State College. She lives in the country between Spanish Fork and Mapleton, Utah, with her husband, Ross, and has nine children, April, Aubrey, Jordan, Arianne, Joseph, Jacob, Amy, Ashley, and John.